GHOST OF
CHRISTMAS PAST

GHOST OF CHRISTMAS PAST

BY

JOHN FINUCANE

www.bookstandpublishing.com

Published by
Bookstand Publishing
Morgan Hill, CA 95037
4741_3

ISBN 978-1-63498-881-0

Cover by
Anna Hickey

DEDICATION

To the relentless search for justice by NYPD Detectives Thomas Gallagher, Sgt. Ronald Heffernan and Lewis Robeson.

ACKNOWLEDGEMENTS

With thanks to:

    Frank McDonald, Detective, NYPD

    Brian Cody, Detective, NYPD

    Patrick Brennan, Insurance Broker

With special thanks to:

    Mary-Theresa Hussey, Good Stories Well Told, Inc.

OTHER BOOKS BY JOHN FINUCANE

When the Bronx Burned

The Usual

Tomorrow, Mickey, Tomorrow

No Irish Need Apply

GHOST OF CHRISTMAS PAST

CHAPTER ONE

CHRISTMAS EVE 1977

In the Bronx of 1977, the drinking age was eighteen, poverty was rampant, drugs were spreading, rents were increasing for buildings that were falling apart, and police and firefighters could barely keep up with the demands of the job. This devastation was no longer limited to the South Bronx. It had already spread to the West Bronx and was moving up to the northern Bronx. It was symbolic of the devastation crossing the country. Some tried to flee—but others just coped with life as they knew it.

That night, Willy Mulgrew, a youngster with a devious-looking smile, and a few of his friends were spending Christmas Eve in the London Lounge, a local gin mill. None of them had yet reached their nineteenth birthday, nor did they have great dreams or jobs. Some had barely graduated, and didn't care about further education. Mulgrew was a high-school dropout. They sat facing the front window guzzling beers, talking sports, and probably taking a hit on the side while staring out on the street watching the many happy, and some gloomy, faces passing by. There were families heading to church, parents returning from last-minute Christmas shopping, and others wandering the streets. Bing Crosby's rendition of "White Christmas" played on the Wurlitzer. One of Willy's cronies sang along with Crosby. These guys were feeling good. They'd been partying for hours.

Willy, the one with the devious-looking smile, had a violent history though still a teen. He wanted to do something exciting. So, he came up with what he thought was a great idea: They'd kill a lowlife. One of his drinking partners declined, "Count me out, Willy.

Killing's not for me," and left the bar. But a couple of them looked interested, especially Bobby Avilla.

Outside, a man with a Christmas tree on his shoulder, secured it on the roof of his car parked in front of Bobby's car. "Hey, isn't that Jake's father, Mr. Mulberry?" asked Willy. But none of them thought to go help him.

And that conversation ceased when several young ladies from the neighborhood walked in. "Good looking stuff. All of them," muttered Willy. "I'd like to get a piece of the blonde," he continued, speaking loud enough for the gal to hear him, to which she sneered, "You wish, jerk. You ugly pervert."

He shot back with a glare, "Screw you, bitch."

But before they could really get started battling, the six-foot-four monster behind the bar warned Willy, "One more word out of you and I'll throw you out on your ass."

Willy shut up, though he gave the bartender a threatening look, then muttered out of earshot of the bartender, "I might have to shoot this guy one of these days." They returned to looking out the window.

At Fordham University, about twenty blocks away, people were gathering for Midnight Mass at the campus chapel. It was 11:45 and the choir was in the middle of a thirty-minute session of Christmas carols. A tenor with a magnificent voice backed by superb harmony was singing "Oh Holy Night". The sounds raised the hairs on many a neck.

Some locals, but mostly students of the college and their friends and family were filling the chapel. Among them was Morris Jackson, a twenty-three-year-old black youth from upper Manhattan. He'd joined two friends, a young man and a young lady who had been waiting for him. They greeted each other warmly. Morris was known as a stand-up guy and very likable. A few moments later

Morris and his friends went inside the chapel to enjoy the sounds of the choir and get ready for the solemn mass.

About sixty-miles to the north in Washingtonville, New York, Detective Thomas Callahan, his wife Helen and youngest daughter, Emma, entered St. Mary's. They too were preparing to celebrate Midnight Mass.

Back at the London Lounge Willy and Bobby Avilla decided it was time to get some excitement—start their own holiday off right, go find *that* lowlife. As they exited the bar, Willy picked up an old army-style duffle bag from a nearby booth. They proceeded to Avilla's car and threw the duffle into the back then jumped into the front of the car and went off on their hunt.

* * * * *

Just a few blocks to the south, another group sat in a bar, John Feeney, who warmly stared into the eyes of his childhood friend, Mary Webber, whom he was extremely fond of, and Mike Nelson and his girl, Babs, were having a few drinks before heading off to Midnight Mass. Feeney and Nelson were two tough kids, who liked a few beers, but were no known to start trouble.

And after that night, these three groups would forever be entangled—and never be the same.

SEVEN YEARS LATER

AUGUST 26, 1983 – "Hello," said Mrs. Feeney into the receiver. From the other end of the line, she heard a grunt of a hello. "Is this Johnny?" she asked, hoping it was and glad to be proved right.

"Yes, Mom, it's me."

"Where have you been, son? You're my pride and joy, and I miss you." Immediately her eyes welled up with tears.

3

"Please, Mom, don't start that. You're gonna rip my heart out," replied John Feeney. He felt the emotional pain.

"We've only seen you a couple of times since you got out," his mother said. She was worried he'd fallen into his old ways. She prayed it wasn't true, she loved her oldest son, but she'd been worn down by his life and all the mistakes he had made.

"Oh, don't worry. I've been hanging out with some friends."

"Where are you staying? Why don't you come home to us?" she pushed.

"I'd only drive Dad crazy. You know with the bad heart and all… how is he?" He could hear his mother getting emotional. He didn't like that. He didn't want to think about what his choices had done to her.

"You know we really miss you." She choked up again. "Johnny, we've seen very little of you over the past seven years. It's no different now that you're out. Our hearts ache for you, son . . . and Mary always asks for you. I think she still has a place in her heart for you."

"And me for her." That was enough for John Feeney. His mother was getting to his emotions. "I gotta go, Mom. I'll see you over the weekend. Promise."

"We love you, Johnny. And so do your brothers and sisters. They're always asking about you."

"I know. And I love you guys too." He paused, muttered quickly as though he had a hard time getting it out, "Sorry for all the pain I caused you," then quickly hung up. He stood in the phone booth staring out at the street, asking himself, *how did I get into this fucking mess,* then stepped out of the booth into the sunlight and went back into the neighborhood social club, an unlicensed bar— somewhere in the north Bronx. He rejoined his business associates, junkies and bad asses all, several of whom had done hard time for homicide. They sat at the bar sipping beers, planning this evening's activity: what bar should they hit? For most workers, the work day was over. Time to stop for a few cold ones. Then it flashed through his mind, the answer to his question, "how did I get into this fucking mess?" His answer was: "Drugs. Drugs. Drugs."

"What have you all decided?" Feeney asked his three junkie cronies, as he rejoined them at the bar. Nelson was quick to answer, "We're going to the old neighborhood. It's Manning's."

"Cool. The old neighborhood," said Feeney. "When?" The mention of Manning's made him think of his brother, Danny. That's where his brother and two of his friends had filled up on beer an hour or so before he lost his life in a car wreck. Feeney had held a grudge against Manning's ever since.

"Let's shoot up and get going," said Nelson. "It's payday. He'll have stocked up to cash the worker's checks. We should get there to catch the crowd."

They proceeded to a back room where they would shoot up, preparing for their dirty deed.

Two months earlier Feeney and life-long friend, Mike "Big Boy" Nelson, were released from Green Haven prison after serving seven-year sentences for killing a drug dealer—they were eighteen years old at the time of the murder—who had begun operating in their neighborhood, just a couple of blocks from Manning's. The last thing they wanted at the time was for their siblings to get hooked on drugs. As John Feeney often said to his cronies, "One junkie in a family is enough." Probably he was referring to himself.

* * * * *

A few miles to the south, but still in the west Bronx, the owner of Manning's Bar leaned against the bar with one foot resting on the edge of the sink, while chatting with a customer. "You Can't Hurry Love" played on the jukebox.

A few blocks away on Jerome Avenue, Nelson pointed out a joint they should soon hit, the Old Bush Mill. "That's next," he said.

A block later they reached Fordham Road—a couple of miles of commercial stores and a constant flow of shoppers and workers— where Feeney and his fellow thugs made a right turn. Just a few blocks from Manning's Bar, they were becoming anxious. "I wonder how we'll do in the old neighborhood?" said Nelson with a feigned laugh.

"Hopefully big bucks," laughed Feeney, his eyes bright with excitement.

In Manning's Bar, chatter filled the background. Somebody sang along with the Phil Collins tune. Manning responded to somebody tapping their glass on the bar, "Hold your horses, my boy," he snapped with a grin." He moved down the bar to refill the customer's glass. As always, there was a buzz about the neighborhood joint, plenty of smiling faces accompanied by laughter. It was a good crowd—especially on a Friday afternoon after work. It was a time for socializing and enjoying each other before the long, hot, weekend started, and for some, time to cash their paychecks.

A loud bang on the front door startled some of those smiling faces. A second bang followed by muffled pounding got some of Manning's clients off their asses heading toward the door. "What the hell's going on out there?" somebody shouted.

That something that was going on out front was confirmed when one of the regulars who'd gone to investigate wound up being slammed in the shoulder by the hardwood entrance door when it crashed open. "Holy crap," he shouted, "They're beating the shit out of each other out there."

With that the bar customers crammed in around the small front window to get a look at the action—three white teenagers were banging it out with a trio of Hispanic teens. Such fights were fairly common since the minorities began migrating northwards into the predominantly white neighborhoods where their cultures clashed with the more conservative, establishment-supporting white community.

"Any of our kids involved?" asked Manning, who still had his foot resting on the rim of the sink.

Right then the car Feeney, Nelson, and the two other addicts were driving in was right across the street from Manning's. "Keep going," said Nelson. "We'll come back after the commotion clears."

"Yep, Giordano's kid," one of the men shouted. "And he's doing very well." He paused watching, then shouted, "Oh shit, the little spic's pulled a knife." The man ran to the pool table, grabbed a pool stick and ran to the door. "I'll break the bastard's arm," he shouted.

The people outside watching the fight started shouting, "He's got a knife, he's got a knife." A couple of older people trying to break up the fight backed off once they saw the knife. The brawlers were flailing away with punches as fast as lightning. One Puerto Rican kid's face was bloodied. Everything was happening so fast. The Manning's customer stepped out with the pool stick. That's when the fight ended. The combatants took off running at the sound of a siren amid threats back and forth: the man with the pool stick quickly stepped into the bar.

By the time the police car pulled up, the brawlers were all gone and the onlookers moved on. In a matter of minutes, the sidewalk was again peaceful and quiet with few pedestrians.

And Manning's was once more filled with people, chatter, and laughter. One of the patrons staring out the front window, commented, "Suddenly it's so quiet out there. Where has everybody gone?" As he left his window perch and returned to his seat at the bar, he missed the car that pulled up at the curb right in front of the window and the three tough-looking young men who stepped out of it.

John Finucane

Then there was another loud bang on the front door. Again, the door slammed open. But this time three men waving pistols barged through the door, shouting, "This is a holdup." One of the thugs followed up with, "One wrong move and we shoot." With the glare in his eyes, the customers knew he was serious.

The startled Manning shouted, "What ... what the hell is this?" Some of his customers grumbled but remained where they were.

"Shut the fuck up, or I'll blow your brains out." With that, the wild-eyed Feeney ran behind the bar and put the gun to the owner's head then knocked him to the floor. One of his equally-wild-eyed partners in crime fired a shot into the ceiling. Fear filled Manning's customers.

Gone were the smiles and laughter. Most faces were pale with fear, a few turned red with anger and frustration.

"Leave him the fuck alone," another of Manning's patrons shouted in his defense. Big mistake: the barrel of a pistol struck the side of his face then across the mouth sending teeth to the floor. Another man stepped forward to defend Manning and was struck in the mouth with the butt of the pistol, knocking him against the bar where two friends grabbed him to prevent him from dropping.

The bad ass Nelson shouted, "Next asshole gets shot." The other gunman, moving fast, ordered the patrons to empty their pockets on the bar. "And hurry the fuck up," he yelled as they rushed along the bar scooping up money, including nickels, dimes, and quarters. They threw punches at some of the patrons; even pistol-whipped a couple of them, for no reason.

They were all hopped up. They never stopped shouting, never stopped spewing threats.

"Now get up," shouted Feeney as he yanked Manning to his feet, the gun still at his head. "Give me the fucking money," he yelled, pointing the gun barrel at the register. "And give me what's in

8

your fucking pockets." Then growled, "Right now." He jabbed the barrel of the gun into Manning's ribs.

"Oh, that hurt," moaned Manning, his eyes bulging with fear, his face straining with pain.

"Payback is a bitch," the gunman muttered, as he cleaned out the cash register, took what the owner had for cashing paychecks, then shouted for all to hear, "You people talk to the police and we will be back." With that, they were out the door. Phil Collins' "You Can't Hurry Love" again played on the jukebox.

One of the thugs fired another shot at the ceiling.

"These guys are fucking whackos," one of the patrons shouted.

What's with the payback's a bitch?" wondered Manning who hurriedly put out a batch of towels for his bloodied customers to wipe their wounds, then called for the police and an ambulance.

One of the customers ran to the window in time to see them piling into a car, driven by a fourth man. With his poor vision, he was not able to get a license plate number.

As far as Johnny Feeney was concerned, the job was a success. He'd taken down Manning, and some of the customers. They'd gotten away with over $8,000, which included the money Manning had put aside in the kitchen for cashing customer's paychecks. They'd be able to party for several days before they would have to hit another joint.

Yes, Johnny was happy all right. He'd be able to drink and stay doped up all night long. But despite his overall celebration over the next few days, there'd be one dark spot. One moment in the morning between waking and the first shot of the day. That's when the image of his mother's face would make him feel remorse for what he did the night before; for the way his life turned out.

CHAPTER TWO

SEPTEMBER 14, 1983 –The humidity was depressing. The air was oppressive and the sky overcast—certainly not the kind of a day the khaki-clad detective liked. As Detective Thomas Callahan entered the office, he could feel his shirt beginning to stick to his back from sweat. *But that's the way it goes*, he thought as he entered the Bronx Robbery Squad room. He was a very easy-going guy. At least here, it was bright with neon lights and air conditioning, unlike in the old station house with its dreary lighting and no AC, except for a few noisy window units. Even worse, the poor parking facilities in the old place had the detectives walking along the hot streets, sticking to the gum-stained pavement. No, he didn't miss it.

The building was part of a newer police station/firehouse complex that until recently served one of America's most burned-out, crime-ridden districts in the infamous south Bronx. It was a neighborhood that would have a lasting impact on these three groups of people: Mulgrew and Avilla, the three detectives, and the Feeney/Nelson gang.

First things first. Thomas Callahan poured himself a cup of coffee, took a seat at his desk—a cigarette hanging from his lips— and pulled out the serious crime reports from the day before. There were always plenty of them. Serious crimes included homicides, rapes, robberies, gunshots, and child molestations. Of course, his concern was robbery. He waved the smoke away from his smarting eyes.

A few minutes later a big man in height and build entered the squad room. Abe Bridgemont, the 7th Division Detective Commander, looked around the busy place before saying, "Tom, got a job for you. There's been a hit at a place I stop in now and then for a few cold ones. Some of our people hang out there as well." Actually, there weren't many police officers remaining in the neighborhood. Many had moved to the suburbs.

"Sure, Cap. Where's that?" Callahan responded, getting to his feet to join his commander. Callahan approached every assignment with a solid focus. He was a serious-minded detective, dedicated to his work, and got positive results in his investigations. His solve rate made him a favorite for the assignments the big bosses wanted taken care of promptly.

"I want the squad to check this out," he said, handing Callahan a printout. "Manning's Bar on Fordham Road. It was held up by four white guys in broad daylight, carrying knives and guns. They pistol-whipped the owner and his patrons. Bad guys they are." It was obvious by his demeanor that Bridgemont wanted these guys caught.

"I know the joint. A nice enough place. A regular bunch of guys hangs out there. I had friends from there, but they probably moved out. A lot of police and firemen used to live around there," said Callahan, making eye contact with Bridgemont. "Do we know who we're looking for?"

"No. Just what I told you. They were armed and were all male whites. And nasty bastards."

"I'll get right on it, Cap." Callahan went straight to Robbery Intelligence to check on recent bar robberies in the Bronx. He also contacted the local precinct to find out what information they had already gathered.

Callahan also needed to research any similar holdups to establish whether there was a pattern. He needed to have all that information available for his immediate boss, Sergeant Ron Hartigan, a topnotch investigator and mentor. With Bridgemont's info, he checked all the files on robberies and felonies in the Bronx, looking for a pattern in locations, in actions, in the number of men, and timing. He paid close attention to anything in the past six months.

Every felony, robbery, larceny or burglary that ever went down in the Bronx was in their records.

An hour later he was informing Sergeant Hartigan that indeed there was a pattern. A nasty bunch was sticking up bars in the north, northwest Bronx and upper Manhattan. Callahan had also determined that the robberies had something else in common; the bars the gang hit were apparently Irish. Hartigan and Callahan, indignant on behalf of their Irish heritage, proceeded to lay out the strategy.

Little did they know where this case would take them. Robbery, drugs, and a seven-year-old murder would come to obsess this team. Friendships would be destroyed between rival detectives, especially those in the robbery squads and the homicide squads. After all, Callahan and his partners were supposed to stick with robberies, not murders. When their investigations uncovered murders, they routinely passed the information on to the appropriate homicide squad.

But that would be dealt with later.

* * * * *

SEPTEMBER 15, 1983 – Detectives Thomas Callahan and his partner, Detective Miles Thompson, started checking out the bars hit by the gang of gunmen. They wanted a quick resolution to this case because of the brutality involved.

Their first stop in the Bronx was Manning's, on Fordham Road, the shopping district that ran across a wide swath of the east/west sides of the Bronx. In the late 1970s the New York City Fire Department had declared Fordham Road the dividing line between the north and south Bronx.

Flashing their detective shields, they identified themselves to the bartender. The patrons paid attention to their entrance, particularly those who'd been robbed.

"We're investigating the robbery that occurred here in August," said Callahan, a brown-headed man, obviously in good shape, while putting out his cigarette in an ashtray on the bar. "On August 26. My partner will also be talking to your patrons."

Manning, a lean six-footer, pointed out the patrons who were victimized. With that, one of the victims got up and hustled out of the bar without finishing his drink.

"Sir, sir," Thompson shouted after him, but to no avail. The tall, gray-haired man never looked back. He simply waved his hands in the air. "I know nothing," he shouted, and was out on the street, nearly taking the door with him.

"What's your name?" Callahan asked the bartender.

"Johnny Manning."

"Who's the owner?"

"I am." Manning puffed nervously on his cigarette. He could not hide his uneasiness at the sight of the two detectives.

"Were you tending bar during the holdup? How many were there?"

Frowning, Manning nodded. He replied, "Three."

"Why don't you tell me how it went down?" Callahan's face was without expression; his eyes showing no emotion.

I already told your guys what happened," the bartender answered, lips pursed. Manning shook his head in frustration.

"That's all right. The local guys did their best, but our boss is taking this extra seriously. I just want to hear it one more time. Maybe there's something we missed, or you forgot to tell us."

Manning said, "You know this area used to be full of NYPD. But with all the minorities moving in and the drugs and crime that comes with it, your guys are moving out of the city. Guess you all think it's safer. And maybe it is. But the rest of us, we've got nowhere else to go."

"You're right," Callahan said, still with that cool, expressionless look on his face.

Manning continued, "Three young guys barged through the door with pistols drawn, shouting, 'This is a holdup.' Two of them also had knives. They threatened to shoot anyone who moved. One of them came right over the bar and put the gun to my throat."

"Did you recognize any of them? Or see anything distinguishing about them?"

Manning shook his head while answering, "No." His eyes darted from Callahan to the patrons. He was obviously nervous fearing he would have to deal with these thugs again. "They threatened to return if we went to the police."

"Did anybody get the license plate?"

"No. Gone before we got a look."

"What else can you tell us? Any familiar faces? Any names mentioned?"

"I know nothing else. To be perfectly honest, I don't want these crazy bastards coming after me," one of them said.

"How about you, sir," Thompson said directing his attention to a gray-haired old-timer sitting nearby. "Can you add anything?"

"No, just that he snatched my twenty-dollar bill from the bar. Cleaned me out."

By that time, Callahan was getting annoyed wondering, *What's with these people? They get their asses kicked, their money stolen, and they won't help us catch the bastards.*

Callahan narrowed his eyes. "Hey, listen, we're trying to get these guys who assaulted your customers and stole your money. How about helping us?"

"If they hear we ratted them out, they'll probably come back and really fuck us up. We don't need that shit, detective."

"Listen to me," said Callahan. "I understand your concern. So, I'll make a promise to you. Give us what info you guys have, and we'll give this place good protection."

Manning nodded and in a hushed tone, asked the detective to follow him to the kitchen. Snapping his lighter, Manning lit up another cigarette. He flipped the kitchen light switch revealing a kitchen no longer in use. "You're not bullshitting me about that protection, right?"

"No. That's a promise," said Callahan, his eyes still narrowed.

"The only information I can give you is this. I think I know the guy. I don't know his name. But I believe he had a younger brother who was killed in a car wreck."

"Do you know where the accident happened?" asked Callahan.

"I believe it was Webster Avenue. Last March."

Callahan's eyes brightened. "Now that's something we can work with."

"Oh, and something else," Manning continued. "One of my customers heard one of them call the other 'Big Boy' or 'Bad Boy' ... or something like that."

Callahan gave him one of his cards. "You can contact me at this number. And you can be sure we'll get these humps off the street."

* * * * *

The next step in the investigation was to examine accident records for March 1983. Callahan and Thompson visited several Bronx precincts looking through the accident reports. Very frustrating indeed, not knowing what precinct covered the accident. It wasn't until they visited the last of the three precincts that covered the north Bronx, the 52nd Precinct, where they discovered that a Danny Feeney was in a fatal auto wreck on March 13th coming from a prom. It was further learned from the 52nd detectives that Danny Feeney had a twenty-five-year-old brother, John Feeney, who fit the description of the man who attacked Manning behind the bar. To top it all off, John Feeney was just released from prison after serving a seven-year sentence for homicide and that another individual, Mike "Big Boy" Nelson, was arrested along with him for the same homicide. Callahan and Hartigan were on the verge of making the arrests, but first photo arrays of the two men had to be put together.

At noon the next day, at the Bronx Robbery Squad, Callahan and his associates, Detective Miles Thompson and boss Sergeant Ron Hartigan, were in an upbeat mood, excited and confident. They would soon be taking a ruthless gang of gunmen off the streets and putting them behind bars. As much as Callahan liked putting criminals away, he had a soft side that sometimes bothered him for having to put away so many once smart kids from good families, who'd gotten caught up with alcohol or drugs. He'd seen too many young men and women wreck their lives and break the hearts of their loved ones. But he wouldn't hesitate to nail their bad asses if they crossed the law.

Callahan compiled photo arrays of Feeney and Big Boy Nelson. The Robbery Squad had access to the photo unit located in the Borough Detective Office right next door to them. It contained the photo of and detailed information about the person arrested with all their felonies and certain misdemeanors. The detectives would go to the files and select five individuals who had a similar appearance and add in the targeted suspect and place them in an array of six photos.

He created them through CARP (Computer Assisted Robbery Program); a computer program where genetic similarities are entered in the computer and the look-a-like faces print out. "Here you go. Use these photos. These perps will do," Callahan said. By noon Callahan and Thompson were on their way to Manning's.

"What bars will you hit besides Manning's?" asked Sergeant Hartigan, as he ran a comb through his hair.

"Man, why are you always combing your hair?" Callahan gave a chuckle.

"Got to be good looking at all times."

"Whoever said you're good looking?" teased Callahan, getting a laugh from the trio.

"We figured after we go to Manning's we'd stop at the Roaring Nineties and the Old Bush Mill," answered Thompson. "If we have the time."

CHAPTER THREE

W hen they returned to Manning's, they were greeted by Johnny Manning and one of the robbery victims they had previously interviewed. Ironically, Phil Collins' "You Can't Hurry Love" was again playing.

The freckle-faced, brown-haired, Thompson asked Manning if they could use his office. Once there, he handed Manning the photo arrays of Feeney and then Nelson. Thompson told him to pick the photo or photos he recognized and how he knew it was them. Manning suggested that Bartley come in to help ID the photo.

"No. That's not how it's done. One at a time. We don't want anybody influenced by the other," said Thompson. "You must be certain." Manning positively identified Feeney and Nelson. Thompson asked him to step out of the room then send Bartley in. Thompson put him through the same process. Again, Det. Thompson was the only one in the room with Bartley. "Pick out anyone you recognize." He immediately identified the photos of Feeney and Nelson.

"Are you certain?" asked Thompson.

And Bartley responded, "Yes."

Several fire department rigs with sirens and air horns blaring sped past outside, momentarily silencing their conversation. "Volare", an old favorite in Manning's, played on the jukebox.

Bartley's jaw muscles tightened. "That's the bastard," he again pointed to Nelson, "that put the six stitches on my face. I hope you get him . . . and give me the chance to put a few stitches on his face."

"We'll get 'em, I assure you. But no good to getting revenge. Your confidence in your IDs makes that almost certain. And being junkies, they won't be leaving the area."

"Before you go, can I get you a drink?" asked Manning as they returned to the bar. He was now much more amicable to the detectives.

They declined his offer, but Callahan added, "Tell you what, when we get the bastards, we'll take you up on that. Oh yes. And you can expect the protection we promised. But don't tell anyone you made an identification. Keep it to yourselves. Call me if anything comes up."

With that, the two detectives were out the door. Next stop, the Roaring Nineties. Today's investigations would be the last time Callahan and Thompson would be working together. Thompson would be promoted to Sergeant and moving on to a new assignment. Together they made a good team. They had made many solid busts, building themselves a good reputation as detectives. Thompson would go to the Bomb Squad, obviously looking for a new kind of excitement. They would remain good friends.

They checked the records. The Roaring Nineties had been held up several days after Manning's. This time eight people were brutalized, both men and women. Several were pistol-whipped, busting lips, loosening teeth, and ripping flesh. Nelson fired two shots at the owner, more of a scare tactic before three of the gunmen—idiots obviously stoned at the time and who were from the neighborhood and known by the owner and some of the victims—attacked him and viciously beat him to the floor. One of the attackers had been drinking there for three hours prior to the holdup. People outside on the street had no idea of the madness going on inside. Two doors away was a supermarket that was still open with people coming and going. Across the street was another bar where hard men from the north of Ireland hung out—that could have been a little too risky for them to rob—a delicatessen, and a pizza shop, all of which were open at the time. These thugs really didn't think their actions through.

The Roaring Nineties was in the busy Bainbridge section of the Bronx, a fast-changing neighborhood once dominated by white Americans—predominantly of Irish, Italian, German, and Jewish heritage. Throughout the 1970s, corresponding with the burning of the south Bronx, there had been a steady influx of Puerto Ricans into the affected neighborhoods. Along with the newcomers came drugs and homicide, which had been rarities until that time. There had been a substantial influx of Irish immigrants in the 80s, many of whom were illegal, but many of who had returned to Ireland after making enough to tide them over.

Both men identified themselves. "We're with the Bronx Robbery Squad. I'm Detective Callahan and this here's my partner, Detective Thompson. We'd like to talk about the recent robbery." Thompson held the photo arrays under his arm.

The owner, Dan Daly, nodded and replied with a simple, "Yes. How can I help you?" while eyeing their shields. Daly's Irish accent was prominent, and so was his caution.

"If we could step over there," said Callahan, as he moved toward the rear to be out of range of the overly attentive customers.

"Okay," said the owner. He shouted to his customers, "Be right back."

"By the looks of you, you must have been here at the time," said Thompson.

"That I was." It was all Daly said, as he fidgeted nervously.

"We have some photos we'd like to show you. See if you can identify any of them." Thompson opened the folder.

Daly was quick to respond, raising his hands as if to defend himself. "Listen, I don't know anything. It's all a blank to me."

"What's the problem? We know who these pricks are, but we have to be sure," said Callahan. Once again Callahan exhibited that straight-faced mien of his. "They've already been positively identified by people in another bar they hit."

"What bar?" Daly asked.

"I'd rather not divulge that. You know, to protect the place."

"That's exactly my concern. If they find out somebody here told on them, they'll be back. And this time they'd shoot me dead and maybe some of my customers."

Callahan assured him, "They won't know it was you. Like we told the others that I'd protect them, we will give you full protection. Nobody will harm you."

With that Thompson started questioning the patrons who had been victimized.

"Please. The NYPD and the Bronx DA's office won't let that happen," reassured Callahan. "You'll get good protection … from opening time to closing." Callahan continued, "This is how it works. Robbery works closely with the DA. It's called the Major Offense Bureau. Several of the very best assistant district attorneys are assigned to it. They take their time and build solid cases and prosecute the offenders to the fullest. To maintain their reputation, they go out of their way to protect victims and treat them with the dignity and respect they deserve."

"That sounds great, but will the cops be coming around too. To keep an eye on things?" somebody asked.

"Yes, in patrol cars and plain clothes. You'll be covered," Callahan replied.

"Look, I know these people," said Manning. "They're bad. Real bad. Desperate junkies and they'll stop at nothing. So please, just let me be."

Callahan pushed. "Look we have to get them off the streets before more people get hurt. Even killed. Like you said, some of them may be your friends."

Daly looked him hard in the eyes. "All right," he said. "But only if you guarantee the protection."

Callahan agreed. "I've already promised you the protection."

"All right then," said Daly. "But first talk to one of the people that were here that night. A young gal who got pretty well beaten up."

"Let's go."

Thompson was talking to an attractive blonde in her late twenties. The woman turned toward Daly. Nodding her head, "What you think, Dan?" she asked while snuffing out her cigarette. "Are these guys okay?" she asked.

"Yes, they are. Two of our own, Callahan and Thompson."

The young lady spoke with a northern Irish accent, a place where the police (predominantly Protestant) are not too fond of Catholics. That's probably why she is here, to get away from the violence with the Brits who still occupy that part of Ireland.

Callahan injected, "My parents came here for the same reason you did. To get away from the Brits."

Daly looked around the bar one more time obviously looking for any friends of the fugitives. He nodded okay to his customer.

"Show us the pictures," he said. Thompson led Daly to the back of the bar to show him the photo arrays in private. Daly identified both Nelson and Feeney immediately. When asked if he was certain, he blurted out, "Without a doubt." He asked Daly to send the young lady to them. She gave her name as Mag Brown. She too immediately picked out the two, tapping their photos. "These are the two bastards."

"I also know the third guy," she said with a bit of a scowl. "That jerk drinks here regularly."

"That's the mind of a junkie," said Callahan. "You got his name?"

"Sure. Derick Mason. He's crazy." She shook her head.

Mason's record included a conviction for homicide for which he served seven years in prison.

* * * * *

During the latter part of the rush hour on that warm, humid evening, the detectives started out for the Old Bush Mill in the Kingsbridge section of the Bronx where they hoped to get another solid identification from the robbery. Wanted to make sure it was the same gang. The streets were teeming with people and cars, and as always, horns were blowing. The Old Bush Mill was a typical pub style construction of the day, part of a row of one-story commercial occupancies, common throughout the city. Many of the patrons were Irish immigrants who were contractors, laborers, or civil servants as were many of their offspring. A typical working-class establishment in this neighborhood. Some of the men were veterans of the Viet Nam War.

Four solemn, middle-aged faces greeted the two obvious, suit-attired detectives; the bartender and a cluster of three male customers in conversation occupying three stools at the far end of the bar. Another half dozen or so patrons lined the bar. Two men threw darts at the dartboard. "Shit on it," one of the two barked. He must have missed his target.

The bartender straightened up and walked in the direction of the detectives. "Good evening, gentlemen. Can I help you?" he asked in a firm voice. Once again, they flashed their shields and identified themselves.

"We're investigating the holdup," Thompson said, then paused briefly observing their immediate reaction. He then asked, "Were any of you here at the time?" as he scanned the foursome's faces. "Or any of those gents?" He nodded in the direction of the other customers.

The combined odor of cigarette smoke and stale beer hung in the air, the not-so-nice smells that only people who rarely frequent bars would find repulsive. The once white ceiling was smoke stained: desperate for a fresh coat of paint. A large standing fan, humming and reverberating like it was going to take off, stood in the corner blowing the fumes around the bar. Televisions at each end of the bar presented the news of the day and recaps of the weekend sports, which nobody seemed to be paying attention to. A popular Glenn Campbell tune played on the jukebox.

"You're in luck." He tilted his head toward the cluster. "The four of us were here when those," he shook his head, his face distorting with anger, "*fecking* whores barged in on us. But the man who was shot is still in the hospital. His poor wife and kids were terribly upset. Hell, we all were. Thank God, he's recovering."

Thompson asked them to join him one at a time at a booth then went through the same procedure with the photos as he did with the others. And like before, he wanted them alone so their identifications would not be influenced by any of the other victims.

The bartender's jaw tightened. "Why did that junkie scumbag shoot Badger?" he growled, and pounded the bar with his ham-like fist. "I would like to wrap these hands around his neck." They were large, beefy hands.

"How do you know the shooter was a junkie? You must have seen him before," said Callahan. "Do you know him? If you do, you better tell us. Don't play games."

The bartender's face flushed. He shook his head. At the same time the trio of customers did not look like they wanted to be questioned either; they looked anxious. One of them kept his beer glass to his mouth; another drummed his fingers on the bar while staring at the countertop. The other guy looked like he was counting the bottles of liquor behind the bar.

Callahan and Thompson were affable, but firm in their approach. Thompson again asked each of the men, one at a time, to sit at another booth and look at the photo arrays, not asking them to ID anyone. Just to check their reactions to the photos. Reluctantly the men looked at the photos, but none of them reacted as though they recognized any of them, even though their eyes told a different story. They were nervous, afraid of what the gang would do if they knew they identified them.

Callahan maintained his cold, passive expression even as he pushed, determined to get these guys to do the right thing. "Come on, will you? We're here to help you. These nasty bastards who battered you all and shot your friend." Keeping his cool, Callahan continued, "Tell us what you saw. If you recognize these guys as the people who shot your friend and robbed you. We'll take care of the rest."

They looked at Callahan but remained silent except for one brave soul. "These people threatened to blow our heads off if we said a word. What do you say to that? Hah, detective."

Callahan assured him, "By the time this is over, if you play ball with us, they'll be sorry they ever laid eyes on you."

Again, the witnesses were afraid to give information about the perpetrators. But like the gang's other victims, once the detectives promised them protection, they eventually came around. One by one, all four of them identified Feeney and Nelson. They also described two others, Derick Mason, and Eddie Stubs. Stubs was the owner and driver of the getaway car, a black Ford four-door sedan. The bartender called the robbers, "...wide-eyed crazies, all hopped up." He continued, "They scared the shit out of me."

"You know, officer," said one of the patrons who spoke with a strong accent, "I may sound like a *softie,*" he didn't look like one, a burly hard-looking man, "but it hurts me as an Irish man, to know that these lads are the sons of my countrymen. Surely, they were good lads with a good upbringing. And look where they wound up. All because of the cursed dope and the people who sell it."

"Ah, Dan, I'm sure these good men don't want to be hearing that. Sure, they've got their own problems," said the bartender, himself a rugged looking man, on the rotund side. He refilled their drinks and asked the detectives if they'd like a drink.

"I'll take a glass of water," said Callahan. "And I would like to hear what he has to say."

"So," the man continued, "There wasn't much of this crap around here before those people started coming up from that God-forsaken part of the Bronx. Hell, that's why many of us had to move up here. To get our kids away from there and all the trouble. It became a bad influence on them. And they started with the gangs and the fighting."

"I agree with him," said the bartender. "And I feel for the parents of these kids taking drugs. What a heartache."

"It's inevitable that the drugs would find their way up here as did the pushers. But no one expected it as fast as it did," said Callahan.

"Or the crime," said another customer. "I have a close friend, a lieutenant in the Fiftieth Precinct. He's often told me that the crime rate up here has increased dramatically since the pushers moved in. Some of our own are acting just like them. That's why we hightailed it from the south Bronx. Some of those PRs were too quick to stick you with a knife. Oh, my friend also said, 'the poorer the neighborhood, the greater the drug use'."

Another customer said, "And they were trying to push the bloody dope on our children. Now it looks like they caught up with us."

Callahan replied, "That's why it is important that we catch up with this holdup gang. They are all junkies. We can get their connections once we get them."

* * * * *

Even though they were also covering other cases, the detectives were persistent in their investigation. They were using the best of their skills to locate and arrest these men who were on the run and had to be tracked down from house to house, from bar to bar, and with stakeout after stakeout, leaving the detectives to sleep in their cars. "Together, we will identify and seize every one of them," Callahan had promised several of the victims. The trio of detectives, Hartigan, Thompson, and Callahan, was driven by the brutality of the gang.

Most of the gang of junkies had previously served long sentences for homicide, including Feeney and Nelson.

The most dangerous of the takedowns was that of Mel Crane, whom they had staked out at his ex-wife's home. Crane went for Callahan's gun, which led to a hard fight for Callahan and his partners with many punches thrown and kicks delivered. Crane fought like a wild animal—smashing up his former wife's furniture—and for a good reason; he was on parole and owed three years for a previous homicide, another drug-related killing. But he was battling another tiger in Callahan who almost plucked out his eyes. The last arrests were those of Bart Connors, the third gunman in the Manning's holdup, who as a youngster was an honor student through his second year of high school, until he got hooked on drugs, and his brother Josh. Ironically, Bart's arrest took place while he visited his parole officer, whom, of course, the squad had staked out.

By early December they had all seven suspects rounded up; excellent detective work. Each of the gang members was charged with at least seven armed robberies in the Bronx, plus weapons and assault charges. They'd switched in and out with availability. Callahan had also passed this information on to Detective Don

Hickman of Manhattan Robbery. With the photo lineups provided by Hickman, several of the members of the gang were eventually charged with several holdups in Manhattan and Yonkers.

As the perpetrators were arrested, they were brought to the Bronx Robbery Squad where they were interviewed and interrogated by the detectives, under the supervision of Sergeant Hartigan, with Callahan being the case officer. They were facing long prison terms. It had been decided that the case would be tried by the Bronx District Attorney's Major Offense Bureau. Maximum punishment would be sought.

It was department procedure that the case be assigned to one detective who is therefore responsible for recording all the details for evidence at a trial and if necessary, who can testify. As was well known, police officers keep memo books for that purpose, to record their activities. Detectives record all activities related to a case on DD5s, which are the records of a case and generally requested by the court to track the progress.

The men were determined to build a solid case against the seven, which they did through lineups and interviews with many witnesses.

"Hey, sarge," Callahan called to Hartigan who was sitting at his desk.

"Yes, Tom."

"These guys are real winners. We finished interrogating the last one. Shit, just like the other fools, he said he was innocent. Even looked like he was gonna cry. Of course, there were no tears. You should have seen his face when I told him he was full of shit. It was like he was stunned. And when I told him he'd been identified by numerous people, he clamped up then shouted, 'Get me my lawyer'."

"Yeah, the big shit wants to see his lawyer," snapped Hartigan, as he pulled a folder from a file cabinet.

"And who's going to pay for his lawyer?" asked Thompson, who answered his own question. "His mommy and daddy, or most likely the taxpayer."

"Hopefully he'll use a know-nothing legal aide," added Callahan with a grunt.

"One thing's for sure," said Hartigan. "They'll be off the streets for a long time, as promised by the DA."

His expression unrevealing as ever, Callahan continued, "They are some bad dudes, all right. When we arrested Nelson, he told me he could have shot us dead. He was hiding behind the drapes in his mother's apartment. Even if he'd been packing, I think I would have gotten the drop on him. I had my protector right here," he added with a slight grin, holding out his right hand as if holding his weapon.

"And I believe he would have," said Hartigan. "He was quick to use the gun, don't forget. He's the one who's supposed to have shot that guy in the Old Bush Mill and fired the shots in the Roaring Nineties. Fortunate for him, the victim at the Old Bush Mill has refused to testify.

"That's him," said Callahan. "He wouldn't rat anybody out. Him, Crane, and Mason. Those creeps detested us. And as Crane said, 'And the fucking system that would lock me up'."

"And Eddie Stubs, who only drove the getaway car. You know why he was the driver?" asked Callahan, who also answered, "because he was a hemophiliac and had to avoid violence because he couldn't stop bleeding. That's the difference between a desperate junkie and a normal person."

Hartigan interjected, "Well at least they believe in the maxim; you do the crime, you do the time," which got a soft chuckle from his colleagues.

CHAPTER FOUR

Between the late 1960s and throughout the 1970s, there were many thousands of arson fires that ravaged the south and west Bronx: several hundred thousand people, most of whom were Puerto Ricans and blacks, were burned out of their homes. Many people relocated to the northwest Bronx, where many of the white families had earlier moved to, causing a huge cultural divide. Unfortunately, with the honest, hard-working people came the drug dealers and the criminal element. Bringing with them a dramatic increase in drug dealing and use by the youth, and its ramifications—muggings, burglaries, violence and too often murder—and that once so-detested word among white adults, motherfucker. No area invaded by the newcomers was untouched. And certainly not the Fordham Road section where Manning's Bar was located, the very neighborhood where both the Feeney and Nelson families resided at the time.

A few years before, early in 1977, a stylish, swarthy-looking Puerto Rican man named Manny Montegro, a known drug dealer from the south Bronx, began operating in Feeney's west Bronx neighborhood. The man with the ghetto accent was going to get rich pushing drugs on innocent school kids. You know, getting them addicted to guarantee him a steady income and the spoils of being a wealthy criminal. From his own experiences living in a south Bronx ghetto, he knew kids were easy prey. He knew too that once they were hooked, they'd do any crime--even become pushers for him— all to get their next fix.

John Feeney wasted no time going after the drug dealer, recruiting his close friend, Mike "Big Boy" Nelson, another tough kid. The two eighteen-year-old six-footers confronted the drug dealer and warned him to cease and desist or he would cease to exist. The pusher's response was, "Fuck you." A big mistake. A few days later they caught him again in the neighborhood trying to push his drugs on the kids. With that, they shot him dead. They were charged with manslaughter and were both sentenced to seven years and released in 1983.

Many in the community felt in their hearts that Feeney and Nelson did the right thing in ridding the neighborhood of a drug dealer. They thought the pair got too much time for shooting what some people had referred to as 'a piece of shit'.

Per the investigation, Feeney and Nelson were not users of heroin or regular users of marijuana at the time of the homicide.

Feeney and Nelson got hooked on drugs in prison, which were readily available, and by the time they were arrested for the robberies, they were hard-core junkies. Through the squad's investigation, they learned from several witnesses that the gang, including Feeney and Nelson, was made up of some very bad people. Some of the witnesses would not talk to them in public; all conversations had to be in private for fear of being found out. The pair had close ties with some members of the Westies (a notorious gang from the west side of Manhattan) whom they met in prison. Several bars on the west side of Manhattan as well as the Bronx were held up by the robbery gang.

Feeney was different from his siblings. He was a tough kid. He would never back down from a fight. And then he was introduced to beer, liquor, and some pot in the schoolyard. It had made him even tougher—or so he thought. Tough enough that he didn't think much of taking Manny down. He was not fearful in state prison. He hung out with the white criminals. He began to think like they did. He began using hard drugs, became addicted and continued using when he got out of prison.

Many of the residents of the north-northwest Bronx had originally lived in the south Bronx and had moved uptown. Some because of improving financial situations, but many because of the changing population and the clash of cultures, and of course, the increasing crime rate. Many of the lower income people became superintendents, just for the safety of their children. People in the south Bronx lived differently; garbage in the streets and alleyways, heavy drug use and sales, drinking on the streets, burned-out buildings, some were quick to pull a knife and use it or just starting fights. It was a rougher version of *West Side Story* –though that had been set in Manhattan.

The changing morality and the declining respect for law and order in the north Bronx were major concerns for many in the community. Why was the nature of the youth changing so dramatically? The answer was simple. Just ask the police officers and firefighters living in the neighborhoods. They warned, "The criminal element among them will mess up many of our kids. They will turn the area into another south Bronx, which was already happening."

In 1979, according to the New York City Fire Department, the south Bronx, which was originally from 138th Street up to 149th Street was at that time extended up to Fordham Road, in the Bronx, a large expansion.

The drug dealers penetrated the public schools. A whole new market for these lowlifes that literally would destroy a whole way of life that would eventually expand far beyond the city's borders, bringing with it murder, burglaries, armed robberies, muggings, arson, etc.—turning young angels into young devils. Drug dealing for some Hispanics and Afro-Americans was considered a birthright, since they felt excluded from the socio-economic system. At the same time, they were destroying many of their brothers and sisters. When they were asked if they tried to conform to the system (education, work, etc.) the answer was usually no.

* * * * *

OCTOBER 27, 1983 -- Sergeant Hartigan's phone rang; he was on it after one ring. "Bronx Robbery, Sergeant Hartigan. Who am I speaking to?"

A weak voice answered, "I want to speak to Detective Callahan."

"Who is this?" asked Hartigan.

"John Feeney."

"What's this about?" Hartigan waved to Callahan to pick up the phone.

"I want to talk," was Feeney's reply.

As Callahan picked up the phone, Hartigan clued him in to the caller and hung up. "Where are you?" Callahan asked.

"Listen, man, I got … I gotta talk to you." There was desperation in Feeney's voice. He spoke in a low tone as if to make certain nobody would hear him.

Callahan picked right up on Feeney's anxiety. "I see you made bail, hah?" He heard Feeney grunt. "What do you want from me?" Callahan asked.

"I wanna deal, okay?"

"You know how it works, John. You have to give us something good, and the DA has to okay it."

Police friends of Feeney's family had approached Callahan and Hartigan to see if there was any way Feeney could get off without time. But of course, when they heard the seriousness of the charges and the brutality, they knew that such leniency would be impossible. The best he could possibly get was a reduced sentence. Of course, that, too, would be up to the DA.

"Guess we can talk, John. What say we see you in about an hour's time? Right outside the 52nd."

"No, no, please. That's too close to home. How about Katonah and 233rd, by the cemetery? I'll be in my girlfriend's car. A black Beetle."

"Sounds good." Then Callahan reminded him in a stern tone, "Don't forget. No bullshit."

* * * * *

The detectives parked right where they said they would. They pulled up alongside the Beetle, more to get a look at Feeney's girlfriend, Mary Webber.

"Wow! What a looker," said Hartigan.

She was a beauty. Jet black hair and light blue eyes. Feeney and Mary rekindled their romance when he got out of prison.

"My God," said Callahan. "What a shame. A real beauty wasting her time with this guy. She must know he's gonna spend time in prison."

Feeney was well disguised in a black coat with the collar up, sunglasses, and a black fedora with the rim concealing his face. He hustled out of the car and into the undercover car. He feared being seen.

"Keep your hands where I can see them," said Hartigan who immediately frisked him. He was clean.

"Do you think I'm that stupid?" Feeney asked, resenting being searched.

"Ask your parents that question, John. Not me," said Hartigan, bluntly. "Besides we frisk all your ilk. Otherwise, we'd be the stupid ones."

Feeney kind of glared at him—his breath reeked of garlic.

Cringing his nostrils, Hartigan asked, "What did you eat, pure garlic?" to which Feeney simply shook his head while opening his window.

They drove to a secluded area in Van Cortlandt Park and parked, well hidden in a heavily wooded area. Callahan asked most of the questions while Hartigan observed Feeney's reactions. Several times joggers ran by. Each time Feeney ducked down so as not to be seen.

"Well, what's on your mind, John?" asked Callahan, watching squirrels jumping from tree to tree. Callahan offered John a cigarette which he took. In one quick motion, Callahan snapped open his Zippo and produced a flame, lighting up both cigarettes, immediately blending the odor of cigarette smoke with the odor of garlic.

"You still got one of those lighters?" uttered Sergeant Hartigan.

"Yep. Still the best lighter in town."

"I don't want to go back to prison," said Feeney. His voice quivered; his hands were clammy. "Is there anything I can do to get off the hook?"

"You won't get off the hook with what you did, but maybe we can get your sentence reduced," said Callahan. "Work for us. Give us major league information. And remember, we only trade up. Give us crimes worse than what you are charged with. And no bullshit." Callahan never raised his voice, always, calm.

"What type of information do you want?"

"Where's Jimmy Hoffa buried?" Feeney's eyes widened. "Where is Joanne Chesimard, who's wanted for killing a New Jersey State Trooper?"

With bulging eyes, head pulled back, Feeney blurted out, "What! How the hell would I know that shit?"

Callahan continued, "You know the DA wants twenty years for each of you." By then Feeney was ashen with fear. "Of course, you can cut that in half, I believe. If you take a plea to avoid trial. But if you roll the dice and go to trial, I can assure you our case is rock solid and wrapped up tight. Trust me, you'll do fifteen years. The DA took a personal interest in this case."

"Oh God, that's a long time. Not good, man." He vented his desperation, grasping the edges of his seat.

"Then what do you know?" asked Callahan.

Feeney hesitated. To rat someone out was against his grain. "I know someone selling drugs."

Smiling, Callahan shook his head and waved his hand. "Not good enough. In your situation that is shit. Nothing."

"I know guys hitting jewelry stores."

Callahan again shook his head. "Still not enough. We want info on cases bigger than yours," Callahan pushed, his eyes still glued to Feeney's.

"How about a homicide? You know anybody who killed somebody?" asked Hartigan.

Feeney shook his head and muttered, "Nope." By now he was shaking with anxiety. "What am I going to do? Give me a break. I don't want to go back to prison. This is killing my mother and father."

Images of Callahan's mother and father flashed before him. Shaking his head, for once he exhibited feelings. "John, you should have thought of those fine people before you did what you did. Before you got involved with the damn drugs. You broke their hearts."

"Please!" He put his hand up as if giving a stop signal. "Don't remind me."

Callahan wanted to dig deep into Feeney's drug experience. How long had he been doing drugs? How had he become addicted? But this was police business. No time for too much sympathy. Callahan often thought of his own parents and how they would deal with him or his brothers if they'd gone wild. He also thought about himself and his wife having to deal with such a tragic situation with their kids.

"Sorry, my boy, but there is nothing we can do for you. That will be up to the judge."

"Take me to my girl," said Feeney. Dejected, he put his hands over his eyes and shook his head.

Callahan and Sergeant Hartigan had met Feeney's parents at the Bronx Court House at the arraignment. Two fine people, they had observed. Mr. Feeney had previously suffered a heart attack. Callahan wondered how he would survive what was ahead for his son. During his conversation with Feeney's parents, he'd sensed real heartache. They'd spoken of how kind and thoughtful their son had been as a youngster, and being the oldest, how he always looked out for his brothers and sisters. One of the girls was the baby of the family.

John Feeney was the only troubled child in the family. The others were successful. One sister was a supervisor with AT&T. His younger brother recently graduated from Fordham College. They also had their share of tragedy. A brother was killed along with two friends in a car accident.

"You know when he started with the drugs?" Callahan had asked the Feeneys. They replied that they first sensed he was messing with beer and sometimes pot in his junior year in high school. Callahan remembered vividly the next words out of Mr. Feeney's mouth: "Next thing we knew he was arrested for shooting a man who was selling dope in the neighborhood. He tried to sell them to his baby sister, our Kathleen."

"By them you mean the drugs?" asked Callahan, for clarification, which he noted in his note pad.

By then Mr. Feeney's complexion was red as a beet; venting pent-up anger. "I know it doesn't sound right, but he did the right thing when he shot that spic bastard. Imagine the fucker bringing his dope into our neighborhood where it hasn't been before … and then try to sell it to our baby." Mr. Feeney was letting it all out, bad heart and all. By then he was almost shouting. "It was one of those fuckers that ruined our Johnny's life."

That was when Mrs. Feeney grabbed his arm. "Take it easy, John. You're getting yourself all worked up."

Callahan again wondered how safe his own three kids were from drugs. *God forbid they ever touch that stuff.* "You know ninety percent of all crime in the US is related to drugs or alcohol," he said. A look of anger covered his face. "So many good kids gone bad because of these rodents who sell them the drugs." Personally, he thought drug dealers were the worst of the worst, that they should all be executed, which of course he knew would never happen.

"Just understand," said Callahan, "just as many Puerto Rican kids are doing drugs. Thanks to the same people."

Mrs. Feeney used the opportunity to plead with Callahan to help her son. As much as he would have liked to, the most Callahan could do through the DA was to cut off a few years, if Feeney would supply them with valuable information about other serious crimes.

* * * * *

A few days later they were back at Bronx Robbery when the phone rang. It was picked up by Hartigan. "Tom, you better take this. It's Feeney." As Callahan was the lead detective in this case, he was handling all the main details.

Yes, John. How can I help you?" Callahan asked, expecting something important. Once again, he sensed desperation in Feeney's voice.

"Can I see you again?" he asked, his voice quivering.

"Why? What's up?" asked Callahan. "You got something good for us?"

Feeney muttered, barely audible, "I think I got something really good."

"Let's meet in an hour. Same place," said Callahan, who then hung up.

"Maybe this time he's got something good for us," barked Callahan. With that, he lit up a cigarette.

"What do we got to lose?" said Thompson.

Once again, they heard the air horns and sirens of the fire trucks next door as they left their station to respond to a fire. A few minutes later, as they cruised west on the Cross-Bronx Expressway, the detectives could see a large column of smoke to their north. "Looks like the brothers in blue got themselves another fire," said Thompson.

"Looks like a goody," added Callahan.

"This South Bronx is an exciting neighborhood for both departments," said Hartigan. "What's left of it."

CHAPTER FIVE

This time Feeney was waiting out in the open, leaning against the Beetle, right where they had picked him up the first time. Once again, they pulled up beside him, once again to get a look at the striking beauty of his girlfriend.

"What an asshole," said Thompson. "He'll never get to enjoy that beautiful woman."

"His mother told me that just before he shot that guy," Callahan said, "he said he wanted to marry her. Look where he wound up."

After the routine search, Feeney stepped into the car. Nods and hellos were exchanged. The squad always presented themselves as gentlemen, when appropriate. These were seasoned detectives, not young hotshots. Feeney was clean as though he had not shot up in a couple of days. He was not the hardnosed punk he was when he was on the heroin.

"Hi, John. First things first. How's your mom and dad?" Callahan was genuinely concerned, to the surprise of Feeney.

"As good as expected," said Feeney, with a surprised look on his face. "Why? Why do you care?"

"Cause I'm a parent. Now down to business," said Callahan. "What's it going to be?"

Feeney hesitated, then looked out the window. "Listen, I am not going to be around for long." Again, he hesitated. "I got the virus."

"What, you a faggot?" joked Callahan, without breaking a smile.

"Fuck you," Feeney snapped, pulling back in his seat.

"Just joking, John. I know you better. Where's your sense of humor?"

"I'm serious. Dirty needles. And I don't need your morbid police humor."

Callahan grinned, as he noticed how thin Feeney was. Again, he thought about the evils of drugs. *So many good people destroyed, he thought to himself.* He then asked John, "Do you think dealers should be executed?"

"As you know, I once killed a dealer. Now I can't live without them," Feeney replied, humbly.

"You got so many people out there bitching and moaning about our drug laws: how harsh they are, sentences are too long, most of the crimes are nonviolent. Nonviolent, my ass," said Thompson.

"They don't complain that half the arrests wind up without convictions, even though the party is likely guilty, thanks to wheeler-dealer lawyers and judges," added Callahan. "How many prior crimes had they committed? How do they pay for their drugs? What's their source of income?" Callahan was getting pissed. He felt bad for the Feeney family, even for John. First, they lost a son in an auto accident, now they'd lose another. This time to drugs. "Do your folks know about this? Because they asked if we could help lessen your sentence."

"No," he said, shaking his head. "And please don't tell them." After a pause, Feeney asked for a cigarette."

"Yes, sure," said Callahan reaching into his shirt pocket, fetching his cigarettes, and giving him one.

"I gotta do something good . . . before my time's up." He paused, looking out the window. "There's this one hump I can't stand. He did a wrong thing to a black guy a few years ago, he shot him ... for no reason. The guy was coming from Midnight Mass, of all places. He shot him dead."

"How do you know he killed him?"

"He used to carry a newspaper article, "The Ghost of Christmas Past". He'd show it around. Always bragging about it. I hate this guy. A fucking coward. Told everybody he shot a nigger."

"Can you spell his name?"

"Sure can, M U L G R E W. Willy Mulgrew. And the guy who drove the car . . . he, he was Donny Santos."

"What was the vic's name?"

Feeney shook his head. "I don't remember. It was so long ago."

"You sure this Mulgrew person did it?" asked Callahan, while staring him in the eyes.

"As sure as there're stars up there," he said pointing to the sky.

"You're not just saying this because you have a hard-on for him?"

"Fuck no. From what I heard many times from those who know him, he bragged about it all the time. It happened by Fordham. The college." He perked up. "Will this get me a no time served deal?"

"That's up to the DA," said Callahan. "We don't make those decisions. And to get a deal, we'd have to solve the case before your sentencing." Callahan paused then continued, "And you know we don't know if this info is good. But we'll certainly run it by the DA."

Feeney did not react.

* * * * *

Although the information about the murder they had gleaned from Feeney was sketchy—he couldn't give them the victim's name nor what year the murder occurred—they felt they had enough specifics to get started, and besides, it could be easy to check out. For the past five years, Sergeant Hartigan had been enrolled in the Graduate Program at Fordham. He'd received his Master's Degree in Criminal Justice the prior year, and was currently enrolled in their doctoral program, doing his dissertation on homicides. He's also trained there for triathlon competitions and knew a number of people at the school. Especially, T.J. Pucci, a friend who'd retired from the police department and now ran campus security. Several years previous, they had worked together as plainclothes men and had made many good collars, one of which included gunfire. Surely Pucci would have the missing information. The three of them drove to the Rose Hill Campus of Fordham College, a noted mecca of Collegiate Gothic architecture, expansive lawns, and cobblestone streets. Hartigan went to see Pucci in his office in the administration building, while Callahan and Feeney went for coffee in a nearby delicatessen.

Pucci was waiting when Hartigan arrived and knocked on the open door. They were no strangers, having often run into each other in the hallways since Hartigan had enrolled in the Graduate Program. Pucci, a lean six-footer in his late forties, said, while pointing to the coffee maker, "Help yourself to some fresh joe," which Hartigan had already smelled.

Hartigan smiled. "I'll do that," he said, while reaching for a mug.

After fetching a cup, he took a set in a deep, soft sofa, almost disappearing. He loved the comfort.

"How can I help you, Ron?" Pucci asked, "Before you fall asleep."

"We're trying to track down a killing that happened here a couple of years ago," said Hartigan. "A black kid. We don't know why or when."

Pucci picked up the phone and called the administrative offices where he had a friend who had been with Fordham for the past five years and would be privy to everything that occurred there since that time. "What was the victim's name?" he asked Hartigan while holding the receiver.

"Don't know. Supposedly he was a young black man shot by a Willy Mulgrew after Midnight Mass on Christmas Eve. He used a .22 rifle."

"Hi, Gloria, this is T.J. I need a favor, if you can help me." After an exchange of pleasantries, he asked, "Do you know anything about a killing that happened around Fordham some years ago? It would have been around Christmas. A young black man died."

Pucci listened then shook his head as he thanked her and hung up. "No luck there," he told Hartigan. Hartigan's disappointment was obvious. "I'm sorry I could not be of any help. But I will continue to check on it." With that Hartigan finished his coffee, shook hands and departed.

The three of them returned to the car at the same time. Once in the car, Hartigan muttered to Callahan, "Nothing." Then facing Feeney, he said, "There's no record of a homicide within the last couple of years. That information you got was erroneous." Feeney stared back at Hartigan and snapped, "I'm telling you, Mulgrew killed that black guy."

"We'll keep asking around," said Callahan, his two hands gripping the steering wheel while looking in the rear-view mirror, checking Feeney's expression.

* * * * *

They dropped Feeney off, right by the Beetle, taking one last look at Feeney's gorgeous chauffer. They then returned to the 48th

Precinct where their Bronx Robbery Squad was quartered. Their first stop was next door to the 48th Homicide Squad. Hartigan spoke to the lieutenant in charge. They searched the files. Again, nothing. The lieutenant reminded him that if they should find any info, to make sure to let him know.

Now back to their own work: robberies. They had many robberies in the borough to investigate and people to arrest. Homicide wasn't their forte. But this homicide was a priority for them.

* * * * *

Because of the vicious nature of the holdups, the Bronx District Attorney had called for maximum sentencing. The prisoners knew how the system worked. If they could provide valuable information to offenses greater than what they were charged with and the names of the perpetrators responsible, leniency in sentencing could be considered.

Over the next few months, the cases came up in court and Callahan dutifully presented the case. In the case of Mike Nelson and Derick Mason, they openly detested the detectives and the system that would lock them up. They wouldn't rat anybody out, preferring to do their time. For them, the sooner they got out of Rikers and started serving their sentences in a state prison the better. The others were not looking forward to the long terms they would get, but the information they were willing to trade was of no value. They would serve their full terms, fifteen to twenty years.

Callahan had learned that Feeney's AID's virus really started taking hold on him about a year into his sentence. Naturally, his parents, siblings, with the exception of one Mary visited him as often as permitted. His sister Ellen could not accept the pain he inflicted on his mother and father, which hurt him terribly. He was transferred to the prison hospital. Over the next months he made his peace with his loved ones, including Ellen, and his higher power, begged Mary to move on, to find a good man worthy of her love. He wished her a large and sensible family. She always listened with tears in her eyes. Two years after being sentenced he passed. Ironically, a few years after being released from prison, Feeney's close friend and fellow junkie, Mike Nelson, was shot dead in a Bronx bar: a hit, it was rumored.

* * * * *

Meanwhile Sergeant Hartigan and Callahan visited one of the better areas of upper Manhattan, Cabrini Boulevard, where Morris Jackson had lived. They wanted to speak to his neighbors and local merchants. They heard good things about him from his school friends and professors, but now they wanted some info from his neighbors.

Once the produced his photo, his neighbors and local merchants spoke highly of him. Said he was friendly, quick to smile, very polite and always ready to help a needy person. Some even said he was a special person. He had formed a group for basketball training for young children that he ran once a week. He always finished off the basketball training with a brief talk about the importance of education to a successful future. Parents often mentioned that.

* * * * *

Callahan put out some feelers but didn't have any responses. And for right now, there were other current robbery cases on their plate. While reviewing the previous day's incident reports, Callahan noted an armed robbery in the exclusive Riverdale section of the Bronx. The report noted that the holdup gang consisted of three black men. A witness got a partial license plate number and recorded that the getaway car was a brown Chrysler. Several days later while checking the incident reports, Callahan noted that a young black man got nailed for a stolen car, a brown Chrysler. Callahan decided they should pay him a visit.

The next morning Callahan gave Hartigan the incident report about the armed robbery in Riverdale, at the same time suggesting that they look into it.

"Sounds good to me, but first we have business at the 52nd," said Hartigan, his face beaming with excitement. "I had a thought about the Mulgrew case. Last night while trying to sleep, I was wondering where to find that file when it suddenly dawned on me. Years earlier, when I was a detective with the 52nd squad, they covered Fordham, not the 48th."

Callahan gave out with a, "Thank you, sweet Jesus." They high-fived each other. "Let's see if Feeney's on the money."

They picked up a couple of strong coffees at a local bodega, then were off through the busy streets to the 52nd in a dark green department car that smelled of coffee and cigarettes.

"This is the best hunch I've had so far," said Hartigan, with a smile. Not one strand of his hair was out of place.

"Then we can get on with nailing this Mulgrew scumbag," said Callahan, while sipping on his coffee. "I love this smell. I wonder what non-smokers would think of it?"

By the time they were on the road, most people were already settled in at work. Their trip up Webster Avenue was a smooth traffic experience considering that Webster was normally a busy Bronx thoroughfare often blocked by Webster Plumbing Supply trucks. When they stopped at a red light, a fire engine pulled up beside them. Callahan saw the number 46 on the truck: Engine 46.

"That's the fire truck next to us," said Callahan. Looking up at the cab, he saw a familiar face in the front cab. "Shit. That's my friend, Fatima. Yo, John," he shouted.

The lieutenant looked down and smiled. "Tommy," he said, opening the side door, and reaching down to shake his hand. "Are you in the 48th?"

"Yeah. Upstairs in Bronx Robbery. And I see you're right next store."

The signal light changed to green. As Engine 46 started to move, Fatima shouted, "Stop by for a cup of our good coffee. We can talk about old times. I'll be depending on you."

"I'll be there. I am sure I will be looking for some information about fires. So, you can count on me."

The area that housed both firehouse and police station was part of the Bronx known as the south Bronx, the arson center of the world at the time where it wasn't unusual to see multiple columns of smoke rising to the sky at any time of the day and fire glows at night.

Proceeding up Webster Avenue from their precinct on 176th Street, the detectives observed many burned-out five and six-story tenements and rows of burned-out stores that lined the streets throughout the south Bronx without reaction. Just a routine sight for these seasoned detectives. They'd witnessed the destruction for many years. It still irked Callahan, another south Bronx kid, when he saw his old neighborhood fall victim to the decay and destruction.

They were two optimistic detectives when they arrived at the 52nd. They were eager to get their hands on the murdered kid's case file. Once they discovered the kid's identity and got the full details, they could investigate and confirm Mulgrew's guilt. But their enthusiasm diminished after they checked through the records and didn't find any unsolved murders on Christmas Eve. They were disappointed but weren't ready to give up. These two seasoned detectives were used to running into such roadblocks. There were plenty of unsolved robbery cases to keep them busy. But this unknown, unresolved case would keep nagging at them, and they'd throw out new ideas every so often.

CHAPTER SIX

NOVEMBER 23, 1983 -- Hartigan and Callahan had to visit department headquarters in lower Manhattan for a robbery division conference at the Office of the Chief of Detectives, a normal occurrence for updating robbery squads on changing policies and tactics.

After the conference, the two detectives stopped at the Chief Medical Examiner's office, the morgue, which was nearby on First Avenue, where a detective friend, Donald Teronney was assigned. Teronney had a hole in the wall office with a desk. On his desk was a picture of his young wife and two beautiful daughters, and a small American flag. On the wall directly behind his desk was a large picture of himself and three of his Screaming Eagle (101st Airborne Division) pals that he served with in Viet Nam—he and his crazy comrades had sometimes parachuted into enemy areas at night to carry out long-range patrols. Hanging prominently next to the photo was a set of rosary beads, the very rosary beads Teronney was wearing around his neck when a dud mortar round landed several feet from himself and his trio of friends. He always credited the rosary beads with saving their lives. Occasionally, a non-believer visiting the M.E. complained to no avail about the beads because of the religious connotation. What the non-believers, atheists, had in common was that they had never served their country in any branch of the military. Hartigan had high praise for the paratroopers and wondered where the guys got the balls to parachute into enemy territory not knowing what to expect.

Of course, Hartigan had his own close-call experiences on the job. When he was attached to the Narcotics Division, because of his youthful appearance he was called upon to act in an undercover capacity, buying drugs directly from large-scale dealers. It was in one of these incidents that after buying a large quantity of drugs from four organized crime members, one of the thugs pulled a gun and placed it in his ear, cocked it, and demanded the return of the drugs—and he was keeping the money, of course. After a distraction, Hartigan retrieved a small automatic pistol he had in his ankle holster and shot the man before assisting his team with arresting the others.

"Don," said Hartigan, wearing a look of desperation. "We're at the bottom of a bottomless pit. We've been fighting Murphy's Law." He introduced his friend to Callahan while exchanging a little police humor.

"I can see that," said Teronney with a grin. "What is it that's driving you two gentlemen crazy? Besides all those robberies going on in that lovely Bronx, that is."

Tilting his head to one side, Hartigan said, "We got a tip from one of our perps and are trying to track down a shooting victim's killer. A black kid shot on Christmas Eve some years back. Possibly sometime in the 70s. Like who knows?"

Teronney laughed. "That is a hard one. There are approximately 2000 homicides committed each year in the Big Apple. Most of the vics are black and most of them are shooting victims. And besides, what are you guys doing investigating a homicide? Aren't you pissing somebody off?"

"This was a case of a good kid being shot dead by a scumbag … for no reason. A white scumbag at that. You could say he was shot for sport. We won't let go until we see it solved. Then we'll turn it over to Homicide," said Hartigan.

"Follow me, gentlemen." He led them through a somewhat dingy hallway to a large room filled with file cabinets. "It's all yours."

They looked at all the cabinets and shook their heads, just as they always did when they visited the M.E.'s office.

"Here we go again. Where the hell do we begin?" asked Callahan, while scratching his head.

They began reviewing the information available, extracting the variables that would help narrow the search. Would the information be broad enough to encompass the murder if it did exist? They decided to examine those cases that happened in the Bronx in December for the past several years' where the victim was a male black and the cause of death was a gunshot.

First, they decided to go back one year to 1982, which gave them several possibilities that were quickly eliminated. None of the killings occurred at Fordham on Christmas Eve.

Then they checked '81, '80 back to 1978. The same result: Nothing. Surprisingly there was nobody shot dead on Christmas Eve.

"Damn it to hell. When are we going to get a break?" asked Callahan. The frustration was taking its toll on them. They were ready to give up. Then for some reason, they decided to start at 1975 and move forward. If that bombed, they could give up on the matter with a clear conscience.

Bingo! While reviewing the cases for 1977, they came across an entry:

DECEASED:	Morris Jackson M/B/21
LOCATION:	Fordham Road, Bronx
DATE:	12/25/77
CAUSE OF DEATH	Gunshot wound to back

"My God! This is Divine Intervention," shouted Callahan, to which Hartigan responded with an "Amen, brother."

"One more thing," said Teronney, as he was checking the file. "He died in Montefiore Hospital on 12/25/77. That's Christmas Day not Christmas Eve."

The detectives looked at each other. For a moment, they looked like two children opening Christmas gifts.

"I don't believe it. Finally," said Callahan. "The murder occurred as Feeney said it did, but he died a day later." Tom lit up a cigarette.

"Yes, we struck silver. But now we go for the gold … the case folder," said a cautious Hartigan, as he ran his comb through his hair. "And for God's sake, will you slow down with those damn cigarettes."

Each time a homicide occurs, a metamorphosis of sorts takes place. As a human life departs, it is replaced by a new life in the form of an investigation. This is a living form of its own that takes the physical form of a case folder. When a victim is discovered, a case number is assigned and a squad of detectives is immediately dispatched to the scene. Photos are taken, witnesses are interviewed, canvasses are conducted, and all physical evidence is gathered. Anything and everything done regarding the homicide is reduced to DD5s, and are filed in the case folder.

As the investigation drags on, the folder gets thicker and thicker. Copies of the various investigation reports are filed in different locations; one copy of all reports are put in the case folder. So, anyone wanting any information regarding a homicide can find it by going to one location, the case folder. That's the way it was supposed to work. But where was the case folder for this homicide? Murphy's Law was still in effect with this investigation.

Since the victim didn't die immediately, the case was classified as an assault. That being the case, it was assigned to a detective in the 52nd Precinct. Then several hours later, when Jackson died, the case was transferred to a homicide detective from the Ninth Division.

Then as the years passed, the boundary lines of the 52nd Precinct changed and the location of the shooting was now located in the Seventh Division.

Also, during this period, there was a restructuring of the detective division that did away with homicide detective squads. This change resulted in the case folder being transferred to the 48th squad. To make matters worse, every detective who had been assigned to this case had since retired or left the department. No currently active detective was familiar with the case.

The detectives had their work cut out for them. But armed with a date and a name, they had a better shot than before.

CHAPTER SEVEN

DECEMBER 15, 1983 – After two more weeks of searching—often on their own time—these dedicated officers finally found the case file in a box marked *Miscellaneous Papers* in the archives in the basement of the 52nd Precinct. They recovered the case folder.

"At least now we know the witnesses and details," said the expressionless Callahan, glancing through the folders.

They started to read the reports that indicated Morris Jackson had attended Midnight Mass at Fordham University on December 24, 1977, with a white couple. He left the service because he wasn't feeling well. His two friends departed with him. After making sure he was okay, his male friend went to a dormitory party and the girl walked with him as far as Fordham Road where they said goodnight with a Merry Christmas peck on the cheek. She crossed the street to her home and Jackson continued to the corner to hail a taxi.

"Per the report, it wasn't long after he parted with his friends that he was shot. About half a block away," said Hartigan. "He was shot in the back and died several hours later in Montefiore."

"According to what I see here," said Callahan, "the squad from the 52nd Precinct focused on two possibilities; a love triangle or the result of Albanian gang violence." At the time an Albanian gang was terrorizing the neighborhood. They were a violent lot, often brutal to the point of killing someone. "But there were no links between the gang and the killing," Callahan continued. He pulled over an ashtray and lit a cigarette. After two quick draws, he rested the cigarette on the near full ashtray. "After that," he said, "the investigation fell by the wayside."

Callahan pulled out of the folder a *Daily News* article entitled "The Ghost of Christmas Past", which detailed the known facts of the murder, just as Feeney had told them. "Guess it's time to get in touch with Feeney. Tell him the good news."

CHAPTER EIGHT

That night a dozen or so friends of Miles Thompson took him out for dinner and a few drinks, to celebrate his promotion to Sergeant. Of course, the detectives Thompson worked with were there as were others, including Sergeant Ron Hartigan, Thomas Callahan, Lew Roberts, and Connie Brown. These detectives had worked and closed many a tough case together. Often times in dangerous conditions with armed perps with nothing to lose, with shots fired.

It was a rather reserved affair for the first hour or so, but after the alcohol had been flowing for a while, the volume of conversation intensified. In fact, a few good-natured *zings* were thrown between the different squads.

"Did you guys hear this one?" one of the men shouted.

"Let's hear it," a few guys shouted.

"A police officer goes to arrest an armed robber," the jokester started. "The robber gets the drop on the officer and empties his gun shooting at him, but misses and when he realizes he missed, he drops the gun and raises his hands and says, 'I give up'." The jokester pauses looking around the room at the many faces.

"What does the cop do?" Thompson shouts.

"He says 'too late' and shoots him."

Laughter poured from the merry group. One of the guys yelled out, "Good for him."

They pumped alcohol into Thompson for sure, and why not? It was his party. They even got him to sing "Danny Boy", his favorite

Irish tune. He had an exceptional voice that was enjoyed by all, including people at the bar. Rightfully so, by this time he was feeling no pain. Finished singing, he went to the jukebox and played a cha-cha. Returning from the jukebox, he started dancing with the music, dazzling on his feet.

"Not bad," said Lew. "But not as good as this dance master."

"Well, show me what you got," replied Miles, his eyes aglow.

Lew leaped to his feet. He joined Miles for a few dozen steps to the laughter and cheers of the brothers.

It wouldn't be long before another member of Sergeant Hartigan's squad would be leaving: Connie Brown. For Hartigan that meant he'd have two partner-less detectives, Callahan and Lew Roberts. Such departures were commonplace due to promotions, transfers, and retirements. In Brown's case, he had outside interests that demanded more attention, which conflicted with his job as a robbery detective. He was moving to a less intense assignment.

As the men continued with the jokes and the zings, Sergeant Hartigan spoke with Detective Roberts about hooking up with Tom Callahan since they were without partners. The first thing Hartigan asked was, "Do you get along with Tom?" Roberts was quick to say, "Sure." And when he asked Roberts if he would mind pairing with Tom when Connie Brown left, Roberts said, "Why not? We'd make a great team."

On previous occasions, Callahan and Roberts had been teamed up by Hartigan, when for one reason or another their partners were not available. For their safety, detectives were not expected to operate alone.

Shortly thereafter, Hartigan asked Callahan the same question, "Can you work with Lew as a partner." Callahan's answer was quick. "We've worked together before. He's calm like myself. And that's what I like. He's a good cop and being black he's not afraid to deal with his own people."

"And a good man," said Hartigan. "Worked his way up. Once the son of a black sharecropper in South Carolina and now a detective with New York's Finest."

"So, when do we start?" asked Callahan. He pushed away an empty beer bottle. "That's my limit."

"As of Monday," said the boss. "I'll have one more," he told the waiter who was picking up the empties.

"Say no more. We'll go see Feeney with the good news," said Callahan.

Lew Roberts and Brown had closed out a case involving another gang of armed robbers terrorizing the south Bronx. They had multiple arrests in which several shots were fired, and a physical struggle ensued with one of the gunmen. Roberts was considered a topnotch detective.

As his supervisor for several years, Hartigan knew his work well and knew that as a team, Callahan and Roberts would have the best potential for solving the Morris Jackson case, which he was determined to see closed.

Roberts had nineteen years on the job, five of them as a detective. Like Hartigan and Callahan, he had done undercover work, often portraying a pimp. He put a lot of time into fighting vice. He enjoyed nailing those humps who got young girls hooked on drugs and then sold their bodies for sex so they could pay for the drugs.

"I'm going to take him home," said Callahan, nodding toward Miles. "Think he's had a little too much." Fortunately, Miles was ready to go home. He did not resist.

"See you in the morning," said the smiling Hartigan, who once again had his comb running through his hair.

* * * * *

Callahan served three years in undercover work. His specialty was armed robbery. He and his team operated from unmarked cars. They would be dropped off in known stickup areas carrying suitcases with weapons and bulletproof vests, walk into a predesignated store, and set up in a secluded location. These locations were determined by previous robberies. Their purpose was to protect the owners, workers, and customers.

On one occasion, a week before Thanksgiving in 1971, when Callahan's partner took the day off, Callahan was with an officer he had never before worked with. He was a little apprehensive. He and his regular partner worked well together; they had each other's back. That night they were in an unmarked car being driven to an A&P grocery store that had been the target of several armed robberies where clerks and customers were pistol-whipped. They entered the store, each carrying a suitcase with their protective equipment, including a shotgun and a carbine. They went right to the storeroom, which had a twelve-foot wall and a wooden platform made especially for them so they could observe from behind a large glass advertisement made of one-way glass.

Outside was a busy street right nearby the stairs to the elevated train stop. There were many shopping stores open for business. Naturally, there were plenty of people coming and going. As far as Callahan and Early, his partner, were concerned, there could be no stray shots should it come to a shootout.

They donned their protective vests and loaded their weapons, then waited.

It wasn't long after that they began to observe two men in black coats with pull caps walking along the store frontage, always looking to see what was going on inside. The next time they walked by there were three of them. Also, a sedan pulled up right out front. One of the three spoke to him.

The employees returned from lunch. The store was again open for business, and the car was gone. Shortly after that, the holdup men entered the store. One went to the phone booth, the other two grabbed a cart and pretended to be shopping dropping food items into the cart. They got on the line manned by the manager. That's when all hell broke loose.

"Stickup, motherfucker! Get the money out!" shouted one of the perps. With guns drawn, waving them in the air for everyone to see, they pistol-whipped the manager busting his lip and eyebrow. Customers started rushing to the back of the store. Others froze in place. The perps with the manager cleaned out each register while roughly pushing the clerks to the floor. The adrenaline of Callahan and his partner was in high gear: they were in what could be a deadly situation. They exited the back door. Early went left to the aisle where he could apprehend the lookout in the phone booth. Callahan worked his way down the aisle in a combat position directing customers to hit the floor. That's when the robber furthest from Callahan saw him and aimed his gun and fired. Callahan saw an orange flash and heard gunfire and returned a three-round burst. The gunman closest to him dropped, gun in hand, the other perp went straight up and came down in a crouch. Callahan was going to shoot again, but there were too many people in the danger zone. Early fired the shotgun but missed his target.

Quickly the four perps were quickly apprehended by the team and their backup. The stickup team was put out of business. They were charged with numerous armed robberies. They were sentenced to long prison terms. People in the store commented on the courage of the detectives. One woman asked Callahan, "Weren't you scared?" Callahan answered, "Darn right I was."

Ironically, just a few weeks later, Callahan and his regular stakeout partner at the time, were in an unmarked vehicle, this time a yellow taxi, driving past the same A&P when they saw three men standing in a doorway, possibly preparing to hit the store. The driver let them out at the corner. They separated, Callahan going first, carrying the vests in a suitcase, walking toward the A&P. His partner followed on the other side of the street with the weapons in what looked like a trombone case. When across from the A&P, Callahan began to cross the street. Just as he reached the other side, he was suddenly grabbed from behind forcefully. One hand grabbed his forehead. The other hand held an object to his throat. He told Callahan, "Give me your wallet, motherfucker. Drop that suitcase or I'll cut your fucking head off." When he dropped the suitcase, he let go of Callahan's head and kicked the suitcase to the side.

When Callahan supposedly reached for his wallet, he was reaching for his off-duty weapon which he carried on his belt above his wallet. Callahan drew his weapon when he saw his partner deliver a blow to the robber's right temple, knocking him out. Callahan's partner had been covering him. The perp's weapon was a large carpet knife.

CHAPTER NINE

ECEMBER 18, 1983 – Callahan and Roberts, who were now a team, were ready to roll. They had much to do: investigate numerous robberies, including finding who robbed the bodega—which would lead them to the killer of the bodega owner—and continue with the Morris Jackson case, on condition that it didn't interfere with their robbery operations or cost overtime. Even though their function was to investigate robberies, not murders, they were determined to solve the "The Ghost of Christmas Past" homicide.

One night on a four to twelve tour, Callahan and Roberts were alone in the office doing reports and manning the phones. They got a call from the desk officer downstairs in the precinct. He stated that there was a guy in front of him named Cash who wanted to see Roberts. Roberts said to send him up. Roberts briefed Callahan before he came up. He said Cash played both sides on the street (good and bad). Whatever it took to get him back on the street. In he came wearing a sweatshirt, even though it was winter. He was looking around as if he expected someone to barge in and grab him.

After a brief exchange, Roberts asked him why he was so shaky. He said it was that new shit on the street he was using. He told Roberts it was called "crack" and that everybody wanted it because the high is intense though short lived. When you come down from it, you get paranoid and you need more right away. He told Roberts, "People will do crazy shit to get it."

Roberts got to the point and asked, "What do you want?"

Cash stated there was a guy on the street looking to kill him over money. He said it was only a matter of time before he did. He had information that would put the guy away. We asked him what he had.

Roberts asked, "Who is this guy?"

"Tuttle's his name. He's crazy. Cash asked, "Did you hear about the Wise Potato Chip Guy murdered on Anthony Avenue?"

"Yes, we did. Why? What do you know about it? If you know the details, you better let us know. Especially if you want our protection. We asked him to tell us about it. He stated that Tuttle always carried a gun. He said the guy made a delivery with his helper. Tuttle was in the store and saw the guy display money and decided to rob him and waited outside. The delivery man resisted and Tuttle shot him through the heart, killing him.

While Cash continued to talk to Roberts, Callahan went into Intelligence, and found the case and made a copy of it and returned to Roberts. The Confidential Informant (CI) provided them with the name of the perp, his description and where he might be found. They provided the Precinct's investigating detective with the relevant information. A few weeks later the investigating detective visited Callahan and Roberts to thank them for the information that led to the arrest of the murderer. Witnesses identified him and the gun was recovered, and Cash was very happy. He no longer feared being shot.

* * * * *

"What do you say about starting the day with a visit to that car thief?" Callahan said to Hartigan, as he depressed the gas pedal. "See if he was involved in the Riverdale holdup."

"Let's do it," said Hartigan, as he lowered his door window.

They began their investigation of the three black men who stuck up the supermarket in Riverdale. Thirty minutes later the new team was parked outside the Webster Projects. They saw that there was an arrest made for a stolen car on Webster Avenue outside the Webster Projects, a series of six twenty-two story apartment buildings—a city in itself—covering four city blocks between

Webster Avenue and Park Avenue from 169th and 171st streets. The team was on its way to interview Wilson Stevens concerning his arrest for auto theft as a link to the Riverdale robbery. The stolen car matched the description of a car used in the Riverdale supermarket robbery in the north Bronx. The thief had stolen a brown Chrysler with the first three numbers on the license plate matching the plate of the getaway car used in the Riverdale holdup.

The trio of detectives, one black and two white, who were dressed in suits or blazers, were in an all-black and Hispanic neighborhood. They were the center of attention as they headed to Stevens's building and when they entered the hall and waited for the elevator, everybody was checking them out. They commandeered the elevator up to the sixth floor.

Young Stevens looked like a clean-cut kid; he did not appear to be a hardened criminal. The detectives introduced themselves and explained the purpose of their visit. "We'd like to talk to you about the car you stole and a little more. We'll go to the station house," said Roberts. "Would that be a problem?"

"No sir," Stevens answered, speaking in a respectful tone.

"You better give me your mother's work number. Just in case we need it," said Callahan, which the kid did. Callahan wanted to contact his mother to get some background information on the kid to help in the interview.

They proceeded to Bronx Robbery where they would conduct the interview. On arrival, Callahan immediately called Mrs. Stevens. He explained why they were interviewing him about the stolen car and the possibility of him being involved in a robbery, at which time she began to cry.

"Your young son seems to be a clean-cut kid who got in over his head with a bad element. That's why we need information.

"Of course," Mrs. Stevens agreed, speaking well of her son. She implored Callahan to help him in any way he could. "He never before got in trouble with the police. And he was always good in school." She sobbed. "I can't understand why he did this."

"Answer my questions. Did Wilson ever appear nervous?"

"Yes. But he'd never tell us why."

"Did he have friends who worried you or your husband?"

"Well yes," she said, hesitantly. "Two tough looking guys. Think one of them was called Football."

"Did he experiment with drugs?"

This question she did not like. After hesitating, she said, "Some nights he came home late. Other nights he went right to bed." She again began sobbing. "We were worried. He was a changing kid."

She paused then, still sobbing, again pleaded that they help her boy.

"That's up to him, Mrs. Stevens," said Callahan.

* * * * *

When Wilson arrived, Roberts walked him into the interview room, sat him down, and got him a can of soda. Roberts presented himself as a gentleman, which the very nervous youngster appreciated. Roberts even shook hands with Stevens and called him by his first name, Wilson. He started off with soft questions: "What's your favorite sport?" to which Stevens answered baseball. "You mean, not basketball?"

"Look at me. I'm too short."

Callahan then asked, "You look like an intelligent person, a college student. Are you?"

"Yes."

"Which school?"

"SUNY at Albany."

"Whoa!" said Callahan. "Big time. Your mom and dad must work their butts off to pay for that. You're breaking their hearts."

Stevens turned away with embarrassment and hurt. Callahan continued, "I would think you are not too involved. And if so, we can help you."

Roberts again took over the interview. "If you were driving that car, most likely you were involved in the robbery in Riverdale. That's bad."

Stevens was thrown for a loop after all the niceties.

"Why don't you tell us all about it?" said Roberts. "This would be very helpful to you."

"Who do you hang out with?" Callahan asked.

"Guys from the projects," replied Stevens, unable to look Roberts in the eyes.

"Were these the guys with you at the robbery?" Roberts looked hard at him.

Stevens did not respond. His hands trembled.

"What are you afraid of? Are you on drugs?" asked Roberts.

"Yeah, crack. That was my initiation to be part of a stickup gang."

Once again, Callahan thought of the horrors of drugs and the scumbags who traffic it. *Another good kid destroying himself. Maybe it's not too late to save his butt.* It was their initial opinion that he was a victim of his environment. After all, his parents worked hard to earn enough money to put him through college.

Roberts shouted, "What the hell is a good kid like you doing wasting your time …"

Wilson's misty eyes widened with surprise on hearing Roberts scolding him about drugs.

"… and your life on drugs?" He shook his head not in anger, but sympathetically. "Were you more involved in this than a stolen car? That car was used in several robberies."

At this point, Stevens broke down, tears rolling down his cheeks. Both Roberts and Callahan felt bad for the kid, hoping he wasn't too involved. *Maybe I can help him,* thought Roberts.

"They forced me to drive the car," an answer the detectives hoped was truthful. They began to lean on him.

"Who forced you?" Callahan pushed, as he continued the interrogation.

"Football and Jessup," he answered. By now the kid was trembling, sobbing heavily, his face buried in his hands. He named others involved and gave the locations of the robberies. "They threatened to waste me and make trouble for my parents."

Getting the photos was no problem thanks to the photo unit. They brought them into Stevens. He was quick to identify Jessup and Football. Now they could close in on them.

* * * * *

"By the way, Lew," Callahan said, "I went through our newspaper morgue checking on the Jackson murder. All I found was more frustration."

Every precinct has a record room, usually in the basement referred to as the morgue. That's where records of all crimes committed in the precinct are kept for many, many years.

"What else is new?" Hartigan replied before going back to their current focus, "Now that the kid identified the perps we'll get photo arrays to the vics to identify their photos, where positive identifications are sure to be made.

"Good. Now we can pick them up," said Roberts."

CHAPTER TEN

Outside the Point Food Market, there was a makeshift altar with a fair-sized polished brass crucifix, and a two-foot tall statue of the Blessed Virgin, and many bouquets of flowers; a tribute to Mr. Matos, who was well-liked and trusted by the community. Several women stood paying their respects.

The distraught eight-year-old son of the owner of the market repeatedly sobbed during the interview. A somber-looking Callahan was conscious of his distress and did not want to push too hard. The youngster's uncle, George Matos, was with him for much-needed support. He explained how important it was to question him right away—the only witness—so that vital information would not be forgotten. Their first question was, "Can you give us a description of the holdup men?"

There was no doubt in young Matos' mind. According to him, two black men entered the store and walked up and down the aisles pretending to be shopping. When they finished, they brought a couple of items to the counter as if to pay for them. Then the smaller of the two men put his soda can down on the counter and pulled out a pistol, then yelled at his father to give him the money. The father sent his son to the backroom to get the money. The father pleaded, "Please don't hurt us." The boy returned with over $400 and gave it to them. "That's when," the boy said, "The small guy said he needed the money for his birthday party. Then he shot my father."

The uncle tapped his chest. "The son-of-a-bitch shot him right through the heart."

Hartigan spoke for the three of them when he offered their condolences. He told the uncle that they'd have to come to the precinct to meet with Homicide to ID some photos. With the interview finished, they left the crime scene.

"After that, I got to get a coffee," said Callahan. For once his suspicious eyes could not hide his anger. "How the hell can you shoot somebody dead … for no reason? Right in front of his kid," Callahan continued.

Normally Callahan, or anyone on the squad for that matter, wouldn't show much emotion over a murder such as this. Their job as detectives exposed them to too many murder victims, some of whom were brutalized beyond recognition. Both detectives were happy that young Stevens was innocent of this robbery.

The murder of Mr. Matos was investigated immediately by Homicide's Crime Scene Squad. A member of the Matos family informed them that one of the perps approached the counter with a few items as a ruse of being a customer. The Latent Prints detective asked if they still had the items. Fortunately, the family had preserved the items knowing well they might be used as evidence and turned them over to the detective. They took photographs, dusted the scene for any prints left by the perps including the can that was handled by one of the perps. Good prints were lifted from the can and sent to Latent Prints whose office was next to Robbery. Both squads worked well together. The can was marked as evidence and sent to the property clerk.

When the Matos boy and his uncle arrived at the precinct, Roberts immediately asked the boy, "Are you sure you can describe them?"

"Yes," said the boy. "I can't forget them." The description he gave was very detailed for a young child. "One of them was really big," he muttered in a child-like voice. "The other guy was small and skinny." He also informed them that the gunman called the big man Football, and he'd seen a gold chain with a large gold football medallion attached. When the son saw the photos of Jessup and Football, he quickly identified them. "That's them, that's them," he shouted in his boyish voice. With the interview finished, they left the station house.

"Sheeeit!" said Roberts. "That's Wilson Stevens's gang. I mean they are his bosses."

Callahan injected, "I'm truly glad to hear that the Stevens kid wasn't with them. We can turn this over to Homicide, which they did, with the explanation that the Stevens boy had nothing to do with the shooting."

The hunt for Football and Jessup was on.

* * * * *

On leaving the bodega, Callahan spotted a delicatessen diagonally across the street where their car was parked. "After that, I need a fresh coffee," he said. "And there's the joint right over there," he said, pointing across the street.

The counterman man must have spotted them coming, like he was waiting for them. "You people are New York's Finest, aren't you? You were checking out that robbery, right?" asked the server.

Roberts nodded in the affirmative and then ordered three regular coffees.

"You got it," the man said, speaking in a pleasant tone. He poured the coffees as he spoke. "There are too many robberies around here." But then he spoke in a hushed voice, "But to have someone shot dead, that's something else. That's terrible." Poker-faced, Roberts responded, "That's the price we have to pay because of drug dealers and their vics." Roberts had the money out of his pocket before his partners did. "This is my treat," he said to the server.

"No, that's on the house. You guys help keep us safe from the guys that did that," replied the server.

"Then keep it for yourself," said Roberts.

While they sat in the car sipping their coffees, the three of them lighting up cigarettes, they discussed the new case and, of course, the stickup they were working on. "The kid's description of the shooter was close to what the Stevens kid gave us. And the name of the guy with him was Football. His description also matched. Only time will tell," said Sergeant Hartigan.

* * * * *

The team checked out recent armed robbery reports of small supermarkets and bodegas in the Bronx. The robbers fit the description of Stevens and his associates. A few days later Football was nailed and brought in for questioning. He said he had nothing to say and requested a lawyer.

Jessup was another story. The team went to his location. As soon as he saw the detectives he took off running. He headed into one of the twenty-one-story Webster projects that dotted the site and disappeared up the stairs. Several uniformed police officers were with Roberts, and they took off after him, with guns drawn. Well aware that Jessup was alleged to have committed murder.

He could be on any floor, maybe in an apartment. But fortunately, the higher power intervened on their behalf. An alert Housing police officer spotted Jessup fleeing from the calls of the police and took him down. They handcuffed him, placed him in the car and took him to the 48th where they booked him. They then interviewed him, which quickly turned into an interrogation. He knew they had him; he was repeatedly identified for the robberies and the murder.

Jessup wanted to reduce his sentence. He was desperate to make a deal. Callahan told him he was identified repeatedly. Jessup knew he faced heavy time. Callahan took his prints and walked them to the Bronx Latent Prints Unit to cover all bases. Detective Baan of Latent Prints told him, "The prints look familiar." The print guys are good. They know prints like some cops know faces and these prints matched up to the ones on the can.

Jessup willingly gave up three homicides that he had solid information on including the names of the murderers, all drug-related.

CHAPTER ELEVEN

DECEMBER 20, 1983 -- "Lew, let's call Feeney. We'll tell him what we found," said Callahan as he dialed Feeney's number. On the third ring, Feeney answered with a skittish, "Hello."

"Hi, John, it's Detective Callahan."

"What do you want?" said Feeney, hitting a sour note. He was still on bail, awaiting his court case next month. His health was holding on, but not looking good.

"Got some good news. Your info about Mulgrew was on target."

"Forget it," said Feeney. "Forget I ever mentioned his name. I ain't talking no more."

"You got to be kidding. We need you to tell the DA what you told us. You can help us put him away."

"No. What I told you I told you and I'm not talking to no damned DA."

Callahan snapped, "Has somebody been threatening you? Let us know who and we'll get him off the streets."

With that Feeney hung up, surprising Callahan. His eyes narrowed, his face tightened, as he stared at the silent phone still in his hand. "You know what," he shouted to Lew, "The fucker hung up. He's done talking." He slammed the phone down, took a couple of deep breaths to calm himself, then paused. "You know we don't really need him now. We have the names of the perps."

"Yep. Two perpetrators with dime-a-dozen names," said Roberts. "And probably hundreds of 'em. From all over the damn city."

"We'll probably have some down time this evening. What say we hit a few of the joints in Feeney's neighborhood? See if anybody knows Mulgrew and Avilla, the Cuban guy."

Before they could visit the Bainbridge Avenue area, where Feeney and his gang socialized, if one can call it that, they had to compile photo arrays of Jessup and Football to show to their victims. Putting together the photo arrays would be easy. All persons arrested for felonies and certain misdemeanors are photographed. A copy of the photograph along with other identifying details are sent to Bronx Borough Detective Office and entered into CARP. Fortunately, the photo unit was right next door to the squad room.

* * * * *

Eight PM would be a good time to hit the bars. By then some of the customers would have consumed enough of their favorite libation to have loosened their tongues. And that's exactly what the detectives wanted: loose tongues tell good stories.

Tom asked that they sit tight outside the Roaring Nineties for a moment. Time for a little reminiscing. He wanted to observe the frontage of the bar that was once known as McChessney's, a reputable family bar known for its large windmill out front and the outdoor seating in the rear yard.

It was shortly after eight when the full team arrived. They were off duty and dressed accordingly, playing undercover. The bar they would check out tonight was ODs, a typical neighborhood bar, diagonally across the street. Right away they spotted a threesome of gents about their age that were obviously feeling good, speaking, and laughing loudly. They sat next to them and ordered drinks and began a casual conversation with them. It wasn't long before Callahan started dropping names. He knew several people from the neighborhood who he had attended high school with. Experience told him that a good way to get on the good side of someone was to tell a good joke when the time was right. And he felt now was the right time.

By then a crowd of at least seven or eight was sitting close enough to where the detectives and the bartender chatted. He wanted them all to hear his joke—the same joke he'd been telling since '61.

"When I got discharged from the service, I got on a Trailways bus in Fayetteville, North Carolina, all set to say goodbye to my home for the past three years. What a relief that was. I took an aisle seat at the back; I was wearing my fancy, tailored, gabardine airborne uniform with all its trimmings—for the last time. Spit-shined jump boots and all. I felt good." Callahan kept everybody's attention by speaking loud, clear, and deliberate.

"No sooner had I taken my seat when a giant of a man entered the bus. He stopped at the front and stared down the aisle, seemingly checking everybody out. His face didn't show what he was thinking."

"Sounds like trouble," someone at the bar said, then laughed aloud.

Callahan smiled at him and said, "That's what I thought too." He then continued with the tale. "The big guy walked a few feet and stopped beside this very Italian looking man. Looking him right in the eye, he said, 'Pardon me, my name is Brown, B R O W N, Brown. And I'm from Texas. I'm six-foot-six, 265 pounds, and I'm white from the tip of my toe to the tip of my head.' The man got up and left the bus.

"The big man moved down the aisle and stopped by a man who was wearing a yarmulke. He also gave him a hard look and repeated what he had said to the first man: 'Pardon me, my name is Brown, B R O W N, Brown. And I'm from Texas. I'm six-foot-six, 265 pounds and white from the tip of my toe to the tip of my head.' Like the first man, the Jewish man left the bus.

"Then the big fellow looked for his next target, staring at the back of the bus where I was sitting. Sure enough, he headed my way and stopped beside me. But he nodded with a bit of a grin, gave me thumbs up as if appreciating my uniform, then turned to the man across the aisle from me and started on him. 'Pardon me, my name is Brown, B R O W N, Brown. And I'm from Texas. I'm six-foot-six, 265 pounds, and I'm white from the tip of my toe to the tip of my head.' Instead of running, the little man looked up at him and said, 'Well pardon me sir, but my name is Murphy, M U R P H Y, Murphy, and I'm from Cork. I'm five-foot-five, 155 pounds, and I'm white from the tip of my toe to the tip of my head'"—Callahan looked at them all making sure he had their attention—"'Except for me asshole; that's Brown, B R O W N.'"

Callahan was successful in that the group and his two partners had a great laugh. But it was all for naught. Nobody knew Mulgrew or Avilla. So, they hung around for one more drink, then bid their farewells and took off. Their work for the day was over.

CHAPTER TWELVE

DECEMBER 22, 1983 – The squad did a search of the records of the people living in the Bronx with the name Santos who possessed gun permits. Only one Santos had a gun permit, a David Santos who lived in the east Bronx. On further examination, it was learned that Mr. Santos had a son fitting the description of Donny Santos who lived with his mother on the west side of the Bronx.

The squad responded to 2600 University Avenue to question a tenant who knew the Santos family. That person advised them that Donny Santos had not visited the family in the past six months. They then visited the building superintendent and asked him if there were any Santos families living in the building. The super, who had only been living in the building for the past six months, advised them that a young woman with that name lived there, who was the mother of several young children. The super advised them that the young woman was known by several last names. Further investigation revealed that Santos' parents had separated within the past year.

They then headed to the Kingsbridge post office and spoke to the manager from who they ascertained that Donny Santos and his mother had moved up the block to 2743 University Avenue.

* * * * *

DECEMBER 29, 1983 -- The squad went to the 50th Precinct to get some final information on the Riverdale supermarket holdup investigation they were finishing up. While there they met an old friend, Ed Hanson. After a brief rehash of old times, Hartigan casually asked, "You ever come across a character named Willy Mulgrew?" The three of them were startled with his response: "Sure

I know him. He's a psycho. If you're looking for him, it must be something racial."

Hanson pulled a Rolodex from his file drawer and turned to the card with Mulgrew's details: address, date of birth, phone number, etc. He further informed them that he occasionally used Willy as an informant who had occasionally informed on associates leading to their arrest, some of who were his so-called friends. He was a big police buff and a fire chaser. They also inquired about Santos. Hanson had no information on him, but he would ask around.

From the Five-O they went to the Riverdale supermarket that was robbed by Jessup and his gang and presented the involved employees, one at a time, with the photo arrays of the suspects. Two of the men right away identified Jessup and Football; the driver never entered the store. Callahan and Roberts then visited several more bodegas along Tremont Avenue in the east Bronx that they were suspected of hitting. In two of the stores where the employees that were working during the holdups, the victims picked the pair out of the photos.

"Looks like these guys want to get caught. Either they're extremely stupid or they were stoned," said Lew Roberts. "I mean, they didn't even try to hide their faces."

By now the squad had built a substantial case against them for at least five robberies.

CHAPTER THIRTEEN

J ANUARY 2, 1984 -- Sergeant Hartigan and Callahan were at their desks checking the previous day's robbery reports when a call came in. Callahan answered it. His expression brightened, even though his eyes remained suspicious. He motioned Hartigan to pick up an extension. "Who is this?" asked Callahan. The voice on the other end replied, "My name is Willy Mulgrew. My friend Detective Hanson asked me to give you a call. I understand you are looking for Donny Santos?"

"That is correct."

"Well, he isn't around anymore. What do you want him for anyway?"

Callahan responded, "His car was involved in an accident. No big deal."

"He's a scumbag," said Mulgrew. "If you want to find him, he's stationed at McGuire Air Force Base. But don't tell him I told you."

"Hey, Willy, thanks a lot," he said, a smile forming on his face, but his eyes remained suspicious.

"Anytime, brother," said Mulgrew, who then hung up. Willy felt relieved, thinking his helping the detectives would remove him from suspicion. Willy spent his days looking over his shoulder.

"Time to pass this on to homicide. Now it's out of our hands. We're robbery, not homicide," said Hartigan. Like his partners, Hartigan would have loved to work this case, to bring about justice for Morris Jackson's family. What made these detectives so determined to solve this case was not only the fact that this young man had always been a good person, but he had so much to offer society and his own community. He had been a *magna cum laude* business graduate of the prestigious Williams College of Massachusetts, a graduate of Cardinal Spellman High School in New York City, and had been getting his master's degree at Fordham University.

* * * * *

JANUARY 3, 1984 -- Callahan contacted Captain L Bellwood, Commanding Officer of the 428 Field Maintenance squad at McGuire Air Force Base. After identifying himself, he stated that the NYPD wanted to interview Airman Donny Santos concerning an auto accident in which there was a personal injury. A description of his car and a partial plate number came up. "This is strictly preliminary. He is not in trouble," Callahan told Captain Bellwood. The Captain requested Callahan to call back the next day at 2 PM, and he would have Airman Santos in his office. Callahan also queried if Santos had been charged with any offenses while in the Air Force.

Callahan's call the next day to McGuire Air Force Base was right on time. He was promptly connected to Santos who evidently was waiting for his call. Callahan introduced himself and explained their bogus investigation of the accident and that they would like to talk to him about it so they could clear things up. Callahan reiterated that he was not a suspect of any kind. Santos, who had nothing to do with any hit and run, was eager to cooperate. Further, he advised them he'd be home on leave starting January 10th. He volunteered to meet them at the offices of Bronx Robbery. They set a date for January 13th at 10 am.

A check of Santos's rap sheet revealed that he had been arrested for possession of a controlled substance, which raised the questions, how did he stay in the military, did he sell drugs on base?

Were they keeping known junkies? Of course, the squad would not address this issue. That was a military concern.

* * * * *

JANUARY 13, 1984 – Donny Santos showed up at Bronx Robbery. Callahan met him outside the station house and brought him up to the squad room where he introduced him to his partners. Santos was very calm about the whole thing. After all, he wasn't involved in any accident, so why should he be nervous? After a few moments, they laid it out, explaining why he was there. Their eyes were glued to his. "You got a problem," Roberts said while making stern eye contact with him. Callahan watched his reactions closely. Now he was nervous. "You were driving around with Willy Mulgrew on Christmas Eve, 1977." He held the *Daily News* article, "The Ghost of Christmas Past" up to his face. "In Willy Mulgrew's words, 'You were looking for a nigger to kill.' You found the young man on Fordham Road as he was leaving Midnight Mass at Fordham College, where your pal Willy Mulgrew shot him."

Santos' face paled. He began to tremble, to stammer. "No, no," he shouted, "I had nothing to do with that. No! No! No!" His eyes bulged. "I already told you, it was Bobby Avilla. He was the driver."

"That's not what we've been told. You drove the car and Mulgrew did the hit," said Roberts.

"Bullshit!" barked Santos, flailing his arms and jumping to his feet.

"Sit down," Callahan warned from his position sitting at his desk with crossed arms. "We're not done yet."

Then Santos whispered, "It was Bobby Avilla. He was the driver," as if he was afraid somebody might hear him ratting out his friend.

"How do you know that?" barked Callahan. "Sounds like a bullshit story. *Whatcha* think, Ron … Lew?"

Callahan pissed Santos off. Again, he was loud, "It's not bullshit," he barked, as Lew Roberts shouted his agreement with Callahan.

"How do you know it was Avilla? How can we believe you?" asked Hartigan, never raising his voice.`

"Because shortly after the incident I was working with him in a neighborhood delicatessen. He told me everything that happened. How they went to the White Castle on Fordham Road to feed their faces. When they finished, they started looking again and saw a nigger kid leaving Fordham. Bobby parked the car. Mulgrew aimed and fired and watched as the guy grabbed a lamppost and slumped to the ground. Then they sped around the corner and parked."

Detective Callahan stopped the interview. "Let's take a coffee break," he said, at the same time asking Santos if he would like a coffee. He then left the interview room. As Callahan was preparing two coffees, Hartigan watched Santos through a monitor, just in case he seemed relieved that he'd been able to hide some information. He didn't.

Callahan returned to the room, gave Santos his coffee and placed his cigarettes on the table with his Zippo lighter. "Help yourself."

"Okay, back to where we left off," said Callahan. "How did they find out he was dead?"

Santos responded without hesitation. "Because they returned to the scene and checked it out. Avilla told me Mulgrew even stood by his victim and asked some of the people if they saw what had happened; if they saw the shooter. Nobody saw anything," He also said, "One person thought the shot might have come from a blue car." He made a point to stress that Avilla was, "really scared and that's an understatement."

Santos even spoke about their personal lives. "Mulgrew was a madman. Everybody was afraid of him," he continued. "He was obsessed with cops and fires and crime." He spoke about how in the past few years when *Hill Street Blues* was on Mulgrew would stay home to watch it and then head out to the London Lounge. He implied that Avilla was subservient to Mulgrew, and that Avilla was a ladies' man and last year had gotten two women pregnant at the same time, and that he liked cars.

"Who are these women?" Callahan asked, maintaining stern eye contact.

Santos knew Avilla's official girl, Anne Bogart, but not the other girl, only that her name was Elsie. He also said he heard from Anne that after they broke up, Avilla had shoved her grandmother down the stairs, while burglarizing her home. The fall had led to a stroke which supposedly caused her death a few days later. Bogart had since moved upstate to her grandmother's home in Roscoe.

Homicide detectives went to interview her after her grandmother's burial, hoping she was still angry with Avilla since their recent breakup. All they got from her was a, "I don't want to talk about it."

But the detectives had their doubts.

Santos continued, "Not long after, she disappeared. It wasn't long before you guys found out she was gone. Right?

"Keep talking," said Callahan.

"Again, your guys went to see her, but this time in Roscoe. But she still had nothing to say."

"We know the rest," said Callahan. "Homicide also interviewed some relatives who believed Bobby Avilla did it." Callahan had checked out the files on Mulgrew, Avilla, and Santos, hoping to find some way to pressure them. But getting the information firsthand from Santos would seal the deal.

"How about Mulgrew? Did he ever tell you about the shooting?"

"Yes," Santos replied.

"When was this?" asked Callahan, while glancing over at Hartigan.

"Just after it happened. I met Willy sometime between Christmas and New Year's. This was also in the deli. He showed me his "The Ghost of Christmas Past" newspaper clipping. 'You see that. I did it,' he said, which I already knew. 'We were driving by and I shot this guy.' When I asked him why he shot the guy, he shrugged. I was pissed at Willy because he involved Avilla. He told Avilla not to worry because when he showed up at the scene, nobody saw anything. They said it was raining too hard to see anything."

Now the squad had enough information to approach Avilla.

* * * * *

JANUARY 15, 1984 – With the information provided by Santos, they headed to Avilla's address in the Kingsbridge section of the Bronx. But as they approached his residence they spotted him on the once clean but now littered street. They were optimistic, expecting him to go along with them to save his own ass. But when they presented themselves to him and their purpose, he replied with a shitty attitude, almost confrontational. Didn't want to know anything and said he knew nothing. The detectives were disappointed. They expected him to cooperate to get himself a good deal by testifying that Mulgrew fired the shot that killed Jackson. But instead of working a deal with him, they wound up arresting him. Callahan observed a blackjack—a deadly weapon—protruding from his rear pocket. They booked him on Criminal Possession of a Deadly Weapon and read him his Miranda rights.

Once in the interview room, Avilla continued acting the bad ass and gave the detectives some bullshit. According to Callahan, he stated, "I carry the blackjack for protection, and I will continue to do so."

After his arrest in the 46th Precinct, they brought him to their office at Bronx Robbery.

The squad used the same tactic on Avilla that they used on Santos. While questioning him about the blackjack, they dropped the same *Daily News* article in front of him, "The Ghost of Christmas Past". That ended his bad ass routine. Just like Santos, he became a shaken man, and when they started questioning him about the murder of Morris Jackson, he put his hands over his ears and shouted over and over, "I don't know what you are talking about … I don't know what you are talking about." To the team, he sounded like he knew a lot more than he would admit. After calming a bit, he stated that the only reason they considered him a suspect was that he'd owned a red Mustang at that time. He also said that he frequently lent his car to people.

"That sounds like bullshit," said Callahan.

"How about Mulgrew? Did you ever lend it to him?" asked Callahan.

"I'd never let him drive my car."

A dead giveaway, thought Roberts. *If he and Mulgrew were in the car that night, he must have been driving.*

Avilla was uncooperative. But since they had no probable cause they had to let him go, once he went through Bronx Central Booking on the weapons charge. Should they need him, they would know where to find him. It was going to take a lot more work and a lot more of their own time to get them.

Of course, they still had Donny Santos who was eager to help.

CHAPTER FOURTEEN

JANUARY 18, 1984 -- Sergeant Hartigan met with his immediate superiors who then set up a meeting concerning the killing of Morris Jackson with the squad commander covering the location of the homicide—then and now—and the Chief of Detectives for the Bronx. After Hartigan laid out all the information they had gathered, the Bronx Chief asked his Homicide Commander what he thought.

The squad commander was adamant with his response, "Bullshit!" He went on to say, "There isn't enough information and probably not enough to ever make a case, and even if they did solve it, no DA would ever prosecute it." The commander also made it clear that they were too busy with current homicides, and he didn't have the manpower available to track down ghosts.

After the meeting, Hartigan asked the head of Bronx Robbery to let his squad work the Jackson case. "Sure," his boss replied. "As I said before, as long as you don't incur overtime and it doesn't interfere with your assigned work." When he got back to the 48th Hartigan told Roberts and Callahan what had transpired. They had no problem accepting the deal. They wanted to solve this case.

After work, the squad met for dinner with Bronx ADA Ross Mantoso, with whom they were tight from working on cases together. The restaurant of choice was the Yankee Tavern, just across from Yankee Stadium. There were still some empty booths in its rustic, Yankee memorabilia-filled dining area.

"Come on. Let's sit by the Babe, the man who built the Stadium," said Callahan. They headed to a booth under a large portrait of Babe Ruth.

Right away they saw two familiar faces from the Four-Eight. Waving, they acknowledged each other. Before they even hung their jackets on the racks attached to their booth, one of the restaurant's most popular waitresses, Carmen Santiago, appeared with menus and a big smile, ready to take their beverage order.

With an equally big smile, Mantoso greeted her, "Hello, Carmen." She was a short, well-endowed, blue-eyed, charismatic Puerto Rican girl in her early twenties. They checked her out as she took off to get their drinks, as Hartigan updated the DA on the Jackson case.

They explained the Jackson homicide and who the suspects were and that they would formulate a strategy to be able to charge Mulgrew and Avilla for the killing and asked for the support of the DA, which they subsequently received. Hartigan explained Feeney's refusal to talk to him but that they had solid information from Santos.

* * * * *

JANUARY 20, 1984 -- It was time to move on Jessup and Football, and their young driver, Wilson Stevens. Three more junkies were going to be off the streets—but the detectives really wanted Jessup.

The squad had built a solid case against the pair for a series of holdups in bodegas and small supermarkets in the Bronx. In one day, they had three out of five owners finger the photos of Justin Jessup and Link "Football" Maples as the holdup men. They still had several more stores to check out that they suspected were hit by them, but for the sake of this case, they had enough evidence to put them away. They also had them identified for the murder of Mr. Matos.

* * * * *.

"Time for a change of venue," said Callahan, getting Roberts's attention. "Let's pick up these scumbags and get 'em off the streets."

Briefly, the smartly-dressed trio of detectives discussed their plans, then signed out. They proceeded to the garage to pick up a car that surprisingly had a full tank of gas. The car blended right in with the neighborhood. It had a few dents and needed a paint job. They jumped in the car and in a few quick turns they were on Webster Avenue. Five minutes after that they were at the Webster Avenue Projects where their targets resided.

Unbeknownst to Jessup, he was also identified as the gunman who shot dead the bodega owner. There was no logical reason for the shooting. The owner had directed his son to fetch all the money and to turn it over to the gunmen, which he did. That's when Jessup shot him through the heart. The squad had also recovered the soda can Jessup had left in the store with his fingerprints on it.

Jessup was a punk with a long rap sheet. He'd done several short terms in Rikers Island for robberies and assaults for drug money. In one of the assaults, he clubbed several people with a baseball bat, leaving one of them with serious injuries, including broken bones.

Roberts interviewed him and found him to be very nervous, which Callahan also observed. Roberts was blunt with him: "We already got you identified on several armed robberies, which means big time."

Jessup still played the bad ass, but he couldn't hide the fear in his eyes. He didn't want to go back to the joint.

"We might be able to help you if you trade up," said Callahan, which energized Jessup's dull eyes. "In other words," continued Callahan, "you must tell us about killings, and give the names and where they happened."

"Yeah, man, I can do that," was his reply. His anxiety diminished.

"So, you must have been a witness," added Roberts, who took over the questioning.

A tech from the DA's office arrived to video the questioning of Jessup. Joan Colley, an assistant district attorney, started the interview with a standard set of questions: How have you been treated? Have you been promised anything? Have you been intimidated? Have offers been made to help you?"

For the live record, Jessup was instructed to repeat what he had told the detectives, which he was happy to do. Of course, his murder of Matos was not mentioned. He proceeded to name the names of the people who did the shootings, giving the times and locations, and stated that he was an eyewitness to them all, at least three murders. He answered yes when asked if they were all drug-related. "Of course," was his answer.

When the DA and her crew were finished with Jessup, Hartigan notified the Homicide detectives. When they arrived, they arrested and charged Jessup with homicide. The alleged killer was outraged. He angrily accused Callahan of setting him up.

"No, I didn't set you up," said Callahan. He had a cheery grin on his face. "There was one killing you forgot to tell us about. Your birthday, when you needed money for your party; when you shot dead Mr. Matos in front of his eight-year-old son. You scumbag." This time Detective Callahan could not hide his anger. His grin disappeared.

The DA was going to *throw the book* at these guys.

"Good. Get some more scumbags off the streets," said Roberts. He continued, "Is everything cleared with the Wilson Stevens case?"

Mantoso replied, "Yes. He's clear. The DA accepted that his involvement was forced upon him."

"Glad to hear that," said Roberts.

"Yes, and give him a chance to finish college," said Callahan. "He has good parents behind him. And he plans to get clean and resume college."

"FYI, Jessup is facing twenty-five to life. Football, as he is called, faces twenty-plus," Mantoso informed them.

* * * * *

"You know we got plenty of time tonight," said Roberts, an inquiring look in his eyes.

"I think I know what's on your mind," said Hartigan.

Callahan perked up. "So, do I. Wire Santos."

"Exactly. Good minds think alike," said Roberts with a wide grin.

Callahan was waiting outside the precinct when Santos arrived, wearing sneakers, jeans, and a worn gray sweatshirt. They went right up to the squad room where Hartigan and Roberts were waiting.

"Donny, you know we really appreciate your cooperation on this," said Callahan. For the record, Callahan ascertained Santos was willing to be wired. "We want to wire you now . . . for tonight. We have to get Mulgrew on tape admitting he shot and killed Jackson."

"I'm ready, willing, and able," said Santos with the utmost sincerity. Santos should have used a strong mouthwash before he showed up. His breath was near overpowering.

The next stop was the DA's office. ADA Mantoso quickly granted approval, and they wired Santos.

"Now, Donny, here is what we need you to do," said Callahan. He had Santos' full attention. "We leave here separately. You go to the London Lounge in your car, but don't go inside until you see our van parked across the street. In other words, don't speak to Mulgrew until we are ready."

Donny nodded. "How I'm supposed to know your van?

"You'll know it. It's very dark in color. Maroon. We'll be right across the street in that hydrant space," said Callahan.

The van was a regular part of Robbery's operation. They were often confined for long periods of time. It was a Ford Econoline that they had furnished with comfortable chairs, provided by themselves, as well as other small conveniences. Except for the windshield, the van had one-way glass all around it, a periscope, air conditioning, and a cabinet in the rear to hold radios for all the boroughs.

The surveillance van was equipped with additional equipment that would receive and record Santos' conversations, which Santos did not know. Santos believed he alone was recording and taping the conversations.

"No problem," said Santos. "If I arrive before you, I'll drive around until you get there." There was a cheeky simper on his face.

Forty-five minutes later they were all in place: Santos sitting next to Mulgrew in the London Lounge and the detectives sat inconspicuously across the street in the unattractive van. They'd lucked out with a nearby spot and did not have to park in front of the hydrant, making them less conspicuous. The conversation between the two was loud and clear, even with all the bar noise: people shouting, jukebox music, even a prolonged belch. Mulgrew asked Santos about the Air Force: what was his job, what was it like? How much time did he have left to serve? There was a brief pause when the jukebox stopped playing. Their conversation resumed when the music started again. But then nothing, just total silence.

"What's with the silence?" asked Roberts, his eyebrows furrowed.

"Must be a problem with the transmitter," said Hartigan, tapping his fingers on the dashboard as if frustrated.

The silence continued for another moment, then broke as Santos and Willy Mulgrew pushed through the door out onto the street. A few seconds later they heard some idle talk and the door slam when the two got into the car. The silence was broken.

"Sounds like it's working again," said Roberts, staring at the transmitter.

Once in the car, they exchanged more small talk, mostly about the neighborhood, including a suspicious fire in the building where Mulgrew once lived. The discussion about the fires seemed to excite Mulgrew. Rumor had it that he started the fires, and many others, but he never acknowledged it. He was a fire buff. Not only was Mulgrew a big fire buff, but he responded to major fires with an appointee of the Mayor who had a city vehicle that he used. He parked at the neighborhood firehouse where Mulgrew's fireman friend worked. It's also the fire house where Lt. Fatima worked before he got promoted.

Santos had previously told Callahan that Mulgrew was also an arsonist, which other interviewees attested to. "These were major fires, two of which he witnessed. On two occasions, almost half the top floor of the apartment building he used to live in was involved in fire. He even knew that his fireman friends were at these dangerous fires. He saw Lieutenant Fatima on the roof with his men cutting holes." Santos said, "He enjoyed seeing the firemen fighting the flames. I think he got his rocks off at fires."

At that point, Santos brought up the subject of the murder. The anxious detectives stared at the speaker. "Did you really shoot that black guy, Jackson?"

"What?" barked Mulgrew, raising his voice to a high pitch. "You serious? I had nothing to with that. It's time everybody knows the truth. I know I took credit for it. I wanted to impress the crew." With that, Mulgrew stepped out of the car and returned to the bar. Santos drove off.

"Crap," groaned Callahan, as he pounded the bench that held all their equipment. "That was a fruitless exercise. Hell, we got problems."

They returned to their office where they discussed the next step. Since they failed to get Mulgrew to talk, they would use Santos to get an admission from Avilla.

"I think I'll call my friend Fatima in the firehouse. Maybe he knows something about Willy and these fires, something we can really nail him on," said Callahan.

"That would probably be a waste of time," said Hartigan. "They have only a hand full of fire marshals and their all new. Doubt they'd know shit about this stuff.'"

"I'll take my chances. Fatima still might be helpful."

* * * * *

JANUARY 23, 1984 -- Three days later they again wired Santos. Avilla was to appear for arraignment on the weapons charge—possession of a blackjack—in the Bronx Court House. Santos was to meet him there, but this time the squad took a precaution. They had an expert from the DA's office bug Santos' car while he was in the DA's office being wired.

"Okay, let's head for the Court House," Callahan said to Santos. "You do know where that is, don't you?" He chuckled, not to Santos' liking.

Santos traveled in his own car. Hartigan and his colleagues Callahan and Roberts took the van, which they parked diagonally across the street from the courthouse. There they watched for both Avilla, whose arraignment should be finishing within the hour, and Santos who should be arriving momentarily.

"There he is now," said Roberts as Santos pulled up in front of the courthouse.

"What do you think guys?" asked Hartigan, as he monitored the action across the street.

Roberts shrugged his shoulders, but said nothing.

"I don't know," said Callahan. "It's hard to trust these people. They spend so much time bullshitting themselves." He watched with suspicious eyes.

"And everybody else," added Roberts. "There's Avilla now."

Santos spotted him and started moving the car in his direction. The detectives heard Santos loud and clear as he shouted to Avilla. And when the two of them met up, they heard Santos offer him a ride, which he accepted. That's when Santos' body wire went dead.

"Look! Once again their mouths are moving and yet we can't hear shit. The transmitter's gone dead again," said Hartigan. "They got to be playing games with us." But this time Santos was unaware that his car was bugged, that their conversation was being recorded. After what seemed to be an exciting conversation, the car moved on.

"Huh. Now it's back on," said Callahan. "Yes, they are playing games." He gripped his hands as if praying then rubbed his chin. He then gripped the steering wheel.

Callahan moved the van into the flow of traffic where he kept a safe distance behind the duo, not wanting to be conspicuous. Santos and Avilla's voices came across loud and clear as they small talked.

"Come on," muttered Roberts. "When the hell's he going to ask him?" That's when Santos brought up the subject.

"Did you guys really kill that guy by Fordham?" he asked. The question sounded almost rehearsed.

"What?" Avilla shouted. "Kill who? I never killed anybody. What the fuck are you talking about?"

"Well back in the day, you and Willy said you killed a nigger on Christmas Eve. Why'd you say that?"

"How stupid can you be?" said Avilla. "We killed nobody. We were trying to impress you guys." He said not another word about the matter. At no time did Avilla implicate himself or Mulgrew in the shooting.

An hour later Santos showed up at Bronx Robbery and turned in the equipment. While that was happening, Roberts hurried to the street to retrieve the bug that was hidden under the dashboard in Santos' car.

The detectives thanked Santos for his help, and as he parted, he shouted, "If I can be of any further assistance, all you have to do is call me."

"Thanks, Donny. You've been a great help. I'm sure we'll be in touch," said Callahan, feigning a smile, even though he was disappointed. Once again, they had nothing. Once again, they had run into a blank wall, but they were not about to let up on this homicide investigation. It had been three months of nothing but frustration for the squad since they learned about the killing from Feeney.

The gloomy-faced trio sat in the office listening to the body tapes, hoping to hear something they had not already heard. But there was nothing of value.

Then they played the bug tape from Santos' car expecting more of the same: nothing. But they were elated with the tape's one exception. They heard Santos warning Avilla not to say anything about the murder because the police had him wired.

So, that's the way it was, said Callahan. "The wise ass. He probably did the same thing with Mulgrew. He warned the fucker."

"Well this changes everything," said Callahan. "At last we can go after them and nail their asses."

CHAPTER FIFTEEN

JANUARY 25, 1984 – After Callahan finished his tour just after 2 AM, he went out to the joint precinct-firehouse parking lot, just under the expressway where it was very dark, to start up his car, a late 1970s station wagon, for the trip home to Orange County, New York. The car wouldn't turn over; instead, it backfired each time he tried to start it. So, he got a jump from a mate also going off duty. After the jump, the car started. In a couple of minutes, Callahan was on the Cross-Bronx Expressway heading for the George Washington Bridge when the car started bucking. Looking in the rear-view mirror, he noticed a small glow. Pulling himself up on the seat he saw flames and smoke pushing up through the seams around the cover of the spare tire well. By then he was on the bridge. He put the pedal to the metal, wanting to get over the bridge.   Through the rear window, he saw flames trailing the car. On drawing near the tolls, he saw a crew washing down the booths with a hose.

Callahan jumped out of the car just in time. The gas tank blew, shooting a large flame from the tank that engulfed the car. "Give me the hose," he shouted, as the flames lit up that part of the bridge.

"No!" the guy shouted, to Callahan's surprise. "You don't want to put that out. It's too far gone," the man with the hose said. "Let your insurance cover it."

Callahan and his family were about to drive to Disney World; he had just replaced the four tires on the car and installed air conditioning. The kids would be devastated.

How am I going to get home? he wondered. Without knowing the extent of the damage, he thought he could put the fire out and continue home. His car was a total loss. He called the 48th and caught another officer going off duty who was heading to Orange County.

It was several years later when he found out what had happened. ADA Mantoso had an informer in his office who was serving time with Mulgrew in the Green Haven maximum security prison who told the DA the story of Callahan's car being set afire. He immediately invited Callahan to his Bronx office to sit in with other detectives as a disbarred attorney told his story about a swindle the mob had carried out.

As instructed by Mantoso, on arrival Callahan did not introduce himself; he simply nodded to Mantoso and his team of investigators and listened as Mantoso finished questioning the informer, Spencer Liebowitz. Liebowitz, the disbarred attorney, was doing time in Down State Prison in Staten Island.

The investigation centered on the milk swindle the mob was pulling off in Brooklyn's public-school system. Through a cover company, the mob was supplying Brooklyn's public schools with milk. They had jacked up the prices.

To lighten his sentence, Liebowitz became an informer for the DA. He gathered information about the mob's involvement with the milk fraud and was now ratting them out.

Callahan was puzzled with it all, wondering what has all this to do with him.

That's when Mantoso asked Liebowitz, "Where were you at that time the scheme was going on?"

When the con said, "Green Haven," that got Callahan's attention. Green Haven prison was situated in Duchess County, New York. When asked, who he hung out with, he responded, "Mostly with the white guys, including Mad Man Bernard, a contract killer, and Mulgrew, who he said was rumored to have killed five or more people." He continued, "They were feared and they kept me alive.

They liked me. I gave them legal advice. I told them how to do their briefs."

"What was the story with Mulgrew?" the DA asked.

"Ugh, he hated some detective."

"Oh yes," prodded Mantoso. Liebowitz raised his voice while cracking a smile. "He hated that fucking guy. He said he got him good." Callahan kept his hands to his face making sure to hide his surprised look.

"How did he get the detective?" Mantoso continued.

"He said he blew up his car in the 80s. And the guy never even knew he did it. Willy laughs his ass off when he tells the story. He even says he's sorry the detective's kids weren't in the car. Guy's a wacko."

Mantoso asked Liebowitz, "How did he manage to blow up the detective's car?"

He replied, "Mulgrew read military magazines and manuals. His favorite one was *Soldier of Fortune*. He said they were good sources for all kinds of improvised weapons."

Mantoso kept him talking. "Do you know how he made his explosive?"

"Yes. He made a small napalm-like explosive. For weeks he had shaved the skins off golf balls and ground them into a fine dust. From what he said, the scrapings, which he packed into an aspirin container, reacted like napalm when ignited. When it was ready, one cold winter night—it was in January, I think he went over to where the detectives were assigned. Mind you, the police station was attached to a firehouse. The crazy fuck went right into the joint parking lot ."

"How did he know the detective's car?" asked Mantoso.

"He had a friend in Motor Vehicle. Mulgrew was a real looney. Right in front of both stations where there was always some kind of activity, he crawled under the detective's car and shoved the device into the guy's tailpipe, then jammed in half a potato. He sealed it in to allow a little air to enter the exhaust so that the car could start and the fire wouldn't die out."

They had Callahan's full attention.

"Then what happened?" Mantoso asked.

Liebowitz chuckled. "I don't know if he followed the guy, but Willy insisted the car burned to the ground on the other side of the George Washington Bridge."

* * * * *

JANUARY 26, 1984 -- When they arrived for work at the office, they were all in good form, even though their workload had increased again: more robberies. Being first in to the squad room, Callahan put on fresh coffee, which came in handy. Each of them had a cup of java in front of them as they laid out their next plan of attack, just like the firefighters next door.

"Good coffee," said Sergeant Hartigan holding a mug with his name on it up to his mouth showing a bright smile and a fine set of white teeth. "We won't let on to Santos that we know he shut off the body wires. Instead, we'll use him to feed Mulgrew and Avilla misinformation."

"The first thing we have to do," he continued, "is put together a list of people who hung out at the London Lounge in late 1977 and early '78."

"I guess we should start with the regulars at the time," said Roberts.

They knew exactly who to contact for help: Detective Steve Bayer at the 46th Precinct, which covered the London Lounge. He had a CI named Jupiter, who hung out in the London Lounge. Jupiter was a black man in his early thirties. He and Bayer had formed a relationship over time. Jupiter provided Bayer with street information on a confidential basis. Though he wasn't close with Mulgrew, he was in on the outskirts of his crowd and would be able to get the details. According to Bayer, Jupiter was the only black guy in the circle but was a shrewd piece of works.

Detective Bayer arranged a meeting between Jupiter and the team. Jupiter was asked if he knew the players: Mulgrew, Avilla, and Santos, to which he answered yes. Then when asked if he had heard about the Christmas Eve killing of Jackson, he said he'd heard rumors about it and "The Ghost of Christmas Past" article, but had never heard Mulgrew say it directly. There had been a comment or two around the holidays about what Mulgrew did to a black man, but he'd never really thought it true.

Jupiter also stated that the word was out in the neighborhood that Santos had put Mulgrew and Avilla wise to the fact that the police had recently been asking questions about that murder.

Putting together the list of Mulgrew's crowd didn't take too long. Between Santos and Jupiter, they compiled a list of approximately sixty names. They divided the names into two lists. The first list featured people who appeared to have matured over the years--they'd started families or were holding down responsible jobs; and the second were the criminal types--the junkies, robbers, burglars, and drug dealers.

The strategy was to interview the people on the first list, obtain incriminating evidence against Mulgrew, and submit the evidence to the Grand Jury, and hopefully, have both Mulgrew and Avilla indicted for the homicide.

* * * * *

JANUARY 30, 1984 -- The team was ready to begin their interviews from List One with a trip to the administrative offices at Yankee Stadium to talk with one of their employees, Peg Liston, who was a friend of both Mulgrew and Avilla. They were informed that she no longer worked there and that she since got married. Her married name was Horgan and she lived on Jerome Avenue. The squad responded to her apartment and spoke to her husband who informed them that she was out looking for a job and that he would have her contact them when she got back.

"On the way back, I'll stop at the firehouse next store," said Callahan. "I wanna see if my buddy Fatima is working. Maybe he knows something about Mulgrew. I know he had worked in the neighborhood.

* * * * *

"Let me out here," said Callahan, right in front of the open firehouse garage door. He walked up to one of the firefighters by the door. "How you doing?" he asked.

The smiling fireman put his hands up like surrendering. "I didn't do it," he joked.

"At ease. Your clean," Callahan joked. They both smiled.

"Would Lt. Fatima happen to be working?"

"You're in luck. I'll get him for you. Who should I say is looking for him?"

"His friend, Tom Callahan."

The fireman yelled into the *bitch box*, "Lt. Fatima, you have company, Tom Callahan."

"Be right down," responded Fatima over the *bitch box*. A moment later he appeared at the base of the stairway.

"Hey Tom. I see you're taking me up on my offer of good firehouse coffee." They shook hands firmly.

"Yes, I will do that. But there's something else you might be able to do for me."

"If I can. But first let's get that coffee." They headed off for the kitchen.

"You worked at the Bailey Avenue firehouse. Ain't that right?" asked Callahan.

"Yeah. Why'd you ask that?"

"We need some information that I hope you can provide us. I know a guy named Mulgrew stops by there every now and then to visit friends."

"Yeah. And he buffs with an assistant to the Mayor who parks his car there," said Fatima. "I hear he's a bit of a nut job."

"That's the kind of info I need from you. Off the record, he's suspected of murdering a young black kid back in 1977.

"His friend told me some weird shit. His mentioned something about a newspaper article, he used to carry around, Something about Christmas. Something about he shot a guy."

"Yes, The Ghost of Christmas Past. What else?" asked Callahan.

"First of all, I think what he said is all bull shit. Said he's killed a few derelicts. As far as I was concerned, in one ear and out the other."

Callahan nodded then asked, "What else?"

Fatima continued, "He talked a lot about arson. That he set some major fires." Then Fatima paused. "As a matter of fact, I remember seeing him on the roof of an adjoining building watching us operating on the roof of a roaring top floor fire. I often saw him around fires of any sort."

"Did you report him to the fire marshals?" asked Callahan.

"I mentioned it to some chiefs, but I never heard back from them. Don't you know we don't have any fire marshals to speak of? We've been fighting the City for years but they always refuse. Rumor has it the pols are waiting until all their landlord friends got rid of their shit properties and collected on the fire insurance."

* * * * *

"The next day they returned to Peg Horgan's apartment to interview her. After formal introductions, Callahan informed her that they had information confirming that she was in the London Lounge when Mulgrew and Avilla returned from the shooting and were bragging about it. Right away she denied being there, but they persisted. Callahan named names of others that were there with her and showed her the newspaper clipping about the killing that was passed around in the London Lounge a few days after the shooting. Again, she denied knowing anything. All along she was nervous; her color was ashen. All she gave them was the name and address of her brother, Danny.

"You sure you don't know anything?" asked Callahan, looking hard into her eyes. He then warned her, "We may put you into a Grand Jury and if you're lying you can be charged with lying under oath. You had better think hard about this. We have solid info to the contrary … that you were indeed there. And I warn you, we are not going away. So, if you know anything you better give it up."

They were mildly deflated as they left the building.

"She knows damn well. I think we'll have to subpoena her," said Hartigan, shaking his head. We got to put her under pressure." He then perked up. "Who's next?"

Callahan pulled the list from inside his blazer and opened it. "Lonnigan," he said. "JP Lonnigan."

"Let's do it," said Hartigan.

They piled into the car. "Where to?" asked Roberts, who was behind the wheel.

"Decatur and 209th," said Callahan, as he pulled out his pack of cigarettes.

In less than thirty minutes they were parked on Decatur Avenue at a hydrant in front of Lonnigan's building, a six-story multiple dwelling, with an NYPD official business placard on the dashboard. They proceeded to ascend the three flights of stairs to the Lonnigan apartment rather than use the elevator. As in all cases, they did not notify him in advance that they were coming. They didn't want them all prepared for the questioning.

Three firm thumps on the door and a shout, "Police Department," brought a loud shout from inside, "Take it easy out there," followed by some grumbling.

JP Lonnigan was a tough street kid who hung out in the London Lounge in 1977 and still frequented it. He was Willy Mulgrew's best friend.

When the door opened, Callahan flashed his detective's shield and introduced himself. He asked the man if he was JP Lonnigan and he said yes. "You mind if we come in?" asked Callahan as he started to enter the apartment. "We'd like to ask you some questions concerning a homicide in late 1977."

Lonnigan was taken aback; very reluctant to let them in yet at the same time he opened the door and stepped aside. "What do you want to talk to me for?" he snapped.

Another tough guy, surmised Callahan. "You're a good friend of Willy Mulgrew and Bobby Avilla. Isn't that, right?"

"That's right. What about it?" Again, he snapped. He stared right into Callahan's eyes.

Lonnigan had a real chip on his shoulder, like he didn't like the police, even though his father was a police officer. The squad wanted to be easy on him for that reason—to give him the benefit of the doubt. He gave them hard looks.

"We've been given your name by several people. They told us you were Mulgrew's best friend and that you were in the London

Lounge when he bragged about shooting a black kid over by Fordham University."

"Who told you that?" He became even more obnoxious, started waving his hands.

"Do you know him? Yes or no?" Callahan pushed.

The three detectives glared at Lonnigan.

"What if I do? Doesn't mean I know what you're talking about." Lonnigan moved his hands to his side with his thumbs under his belt.

Callahan maintained his cool, as always. "Your good friend told you he shot and killed someone? He showed you a newspaper article, "The Ghost of Christmas Past", and said he killed that guy, right?"

"I don't know shit and that's all I got to say. Now get out of my apartment." He started for the door only to be intercepted by Roberts. "The next time we see you we won't be so nice. This one is on your father."

Then Callahan warned, "We know better, and we are not going away. We'll have you tell your story to a Grand Jury."

"Fuck you and your Grand Jury," he barked as he opened the door, then thumbed them, shouting, "Out. Get out." Lonnigan slammed the door behind them.

"He needs his ass kicked," said Hartigan while checking his watch. "We got time for one more. Let's check out Bonner. He should be in his shop by now."

Bonner was a successful business man with a dozen employees and at least six vans on the road. Bonner was about to enter the shop when the detectives arrived. "Mr. Bonner," Callahan shouted. "We're with the NYPD." He flashed his shield. "We'd like to ask you a few questions. Do you mind if we come in?"

"Yeah sure. Follow me. They followed him into the store. His office manager, a stern-looking, petite brown-haired woman in her late thirties, was just leaving for the day. She was evidently taken aback. "Everything okay, George?" she asked; her eyes wide with surprise.

"No problem. Just lock up on the way out. I'll see you in the morning."

Callahan stated their purpose. On the mention of Mulgrew and the homicide, Bonner's ruddy complexion turned pale. His trepidation was obvious.

Roberts started the questioning with, "Do you know Willy Mulgrew? Did you hang out in the London Lounge during late 1977?" To these questions, he answered yes. He also answered yes when asked if he was around there during the Christmas holidays in 1977. But when asked if he knew anything about Mulgrew and Avilla having anything to do with the Jackson killing, or if he was shown the news clipping by Mulgrew, he very casually stared into Callahan's eyes, shook his head, and said, "No sir." What they did get out of Bonner was a confirmation of the names supplied by Santos and Jupiter.

No longer was this case a simple challenge for them. It was now an obsession. They brought it home with them, constantly thinking about it; constantly thinking of how to nail Mulgrew and Avilla. And they sensed they were again being stonewalled. Like all these people had been tipped off to expect a visit from the NYPD.

The following day Callahan got a call from Ann Horgan's brother Danny, who was only twelve-years-old at the time of the shooting. During the interview, it was learned that Horgan currently frequented the London Lounge where Mulgrew still hung out. Callahan advised him that if necessary he would contact him at a future date.

That night George Bonner went to the London Lounge with one purpose in mind, to spread the word: The police are determined to hang Mulgrew and Avilla. There he met up with JP Lonnigan and Ann Horgan, who like himself, had been interviewed by Hartigan's squad. It seemed like every time Mulgrew's friends visited the London Lounge somebody else had been visited by the detectives.

Lonnigan thought it would be a good idea to have a meeting of all the main characters to make sure everybody told the same story. A good idea if it worked. They all agreed. They knew this was a serious investigation that was not going away, just as Callahan, Roberts, and Hartigan had already made perfectly clear to those they interviewed.

Word spread quickly that the police were on the hunt for witnesses against Mulgrew and Avilla. Word also spread that the boys in blue had the names of the people who hung out in the London Lounge at the time and since and that they'd all be getting a visit.

Lonnigan contacted Mulgrew who contacted Avilla, advising him about the meeting. Collectively they decided who should be at the meeting. They made sure all concerned were contacted.

The following Friday night a meeting was held in Lonnigan's apartment. It was like a mini-bar, beer was flowing; cigarette smoke weaved through the air. The beer drinking helped calm the nerves of Mulgrew and his bar friends, including JP Lonnigan who continued to put on the *I couldn't care less* front. Others at the meeting included Lonnigan's wife Nancy, Willy Mulgrew, Bobby Avilla, Donny Santos, Terry Sloan, Ann Horgan, George Bonner, and Tony Moore. Moore was already feeling no pain when he arrived, with a case of beer under his arm.

They discussed strategy, stressing that if everybody continuously denied knowing about the homicide, it would go away. They would be silent and refuse to cooperate with the detectives.

They discussed the questions presented to those already interviewed by the detectives. They also came up with several questions they figured might be asked, such as: Did Mulgrew or Avilla admit to them that they killed Jackson? It was agreed by all that they would say nothing to implicate Mulgrew and Avilla. Moore, who was *well on it* by the meeting's close, closed the meeting with the comment, "You know, like the Ricans say, 'I know nutting, mister,'" which did not get much of a laugh.

CHAPTER SIXTEEN

JANUARY 31, 1984 – After work, the trio of detectives stopped at Sloan's auto repair shop. Sloan was an ace car mechanic with a good business. He was married with a young family. The detectives flashed their badges and stated their business. Sloan did not look surprised.

They asked him the standard questions: Did Willy Mulgrew or Bobby Avilla ever tell you about a homicide they committed, to which he answered, "Not that I can remember." Hartigan wondered to himself, how could he forget something like that?

They also asked him about the general atmosphere at the bar in '77. Hartigan went over the names of people who hung out there and who were the big drinkers and dopers. Sloan added that not everybody was into the drug scene.

They asked him about Mulgrew: What kind of a guy was he? At first, he hesitated, remained silent. Roberts pushed him. "We know you hung around there ... that you knew Mulgrew well." Finally, Sloan gave up some information, but not what they were looking for. Instead of talking about what he was supposed to know about Mulgrew, he spoke about what had been rumored about him: that on occasion Mulgrew traveled the subways or Van Cortlandt Park in the early hours of the morning looking for derelicts to shoot. Whether he had shot anybody, he did not know. Sloan also said, "He sometimes disguised himself as a woman."

By then Sloan was perspiring, his hands seemed to tremble, which of course the seasoned detectives took in. They knew he knew more than he was admitting. Besides, others had provided the same information about the rumored killings.

Callahan asked him, "Did Mulgrew have any handles? You know, nicknames."

After a short hesitation, he said yes. "Some people called him, Pyro. But don't ask me why because I don't know." The odds were that he knew well why he was called Pyro. Look gents, I got to get to work."

"A word to the wise," said Callahan. "We will not be finished with you or your friends until this murder is solved. And we know who did it. It's only a matter of time."

CHAPTER SEVENTEEN

F EBRUARY 2, 1984 – Sergeant Hartigan was going through the original case file of the Jackson murder accumulated by the 52nd Precinct detectives and uncovered one interview report he found very interesting. The interviewee's name was Mike Fahey, a young seminarian at the time. None of the original detectives who interviewed him right after the murder on Christmas Day, 1977, were still on the job.

"Gentlemen, our next stop will be Fordham University," said Hartigan. "I want to track down a Father Mike Fahey. I think he can be helpful. Seems he heard the shooting and saw a car drive away. That's about all that looks helpful. At least for now."

They were back at the administration building on the Fordham campus, this time seeking a meeting with Father Fahey, who they learned at that time, was residing in Micronesia in the western Pacific, thousands of miles from the campus. Fortunately, the priest had business in Massachusetts in a couple of weeks and was stopping by Fordham. Hartigan arranged for a meeting.

* * * * *

FEBRUARY 22, 1984 -- The interview took place in the Murray Weigel Hall at Fordham University. One thing Hartigan wanted to know was if the priest could identify Mulgrew and Avilla, now that they had the alleged killers in their sights.

As Father Fahey recalled it, at about 2 AM, he was standing outside Murray Weigel Hall waiting for a ride. He saw a red two-door sedan stop abruptly at the corner of Bathgate and Fordham at which time he heard "two pops". The car then continued passing right in front of him. Fahey recalled that when the two occupants saw him—he was wearing clerical garb—they looked shocked, surprised that anyone might have seen them. He stated, "I saw one man driving the car and another sitting in the back seat." He described the driver as eighteen to twenty-five-years-old with an olive complexion and long dark hair. The man in the back seat he described as the same age, with a white complexion, and longer, slightly lighter hair. When the priest testified at the trial, he positively identified Mulgrew's picture, saying it matched the face he saw looking out of the side window of the car.

After the car passed, he thought he heard somebody crying or moaning, which he thought came from the apartment building across the street. He didn't give it much thought as he was becoming impatient waiting for his ride. He returned to Murray Weigel Hall. Some of the other seminarians were rushing out onto the street saying somebody was injured and was lying outside. He joined the others who tried to help the man.

Over the next few weeks, when their normal workload of robbery cases permitted, they interviewed several more individuals from the first list. They kept running into the group's code of silence, which didn't bode well for the investigators and their plans. They had hoped to catch them off guard, to witness their first impressions, to study their facial expressions. But no, they were all prepared.

A name that kept cropping up during these interviews was Arnie Schuster, a close friend of Mulgrew in 1977, who had disappeared from the crowd about five years earlier. It was rumored that he might be a police officer somewhere in Florida, possibly in the Miami area, which is where Callahan began contacting the different police departments.

He contacted the office of the Commander of the Florida State Police which provided him with contact information for over 170 state, town, and city police departments that policed many of the almost 900 municipalities in the state. It would be one hell of a job, they figured, but they were determined to see it through. Once again, in between regular investigations and on down time, they would call a couple of departments and ask for Officer Arnie Schuster.

After several days and dozens of calls, Callahan contacted the right police department. He was on his third call of the day when he asked to speak to Officer Arnie Schuster. The dispatcher replied, "No," like all the other times, however, this time the dispatcher added, "But he's due in tomorrow for a four to twelve."

"Thank you," said the wide-eyed Callahan as he hung up the phone. "I think we hit pay dirt! I just spoke to the Miami North dispatcher. He said Schuster will be in tomorrow."

"*Smoking*, baby," said Roberts. "If this is the real Arnie Schuster and he's on the job, he has no choice but to cooperate. I think our fortune is about to change."

The next day, shortly after 4 PM, Callahan was on the phone again, just as the Miami North's tour started. He wanted to get Schuster before he went out on patrol. Sure enough, it was Schuster himself that answered the phone. Callahan introduced himself and explained why he was calling, making perfectly clear that they knew he was aware of what Mulgrew and Avilla had done.

Schuster asked, "Can I call you back?" Right away Callahan sensed Schuster's gut feelings, that same anxiety and fear that overcame Santos and Avilla when they were confronted with the Jackson murder.

Callahan agreed to let Schuster call him and gave him the phone number where he could be reached, then waited and waited for more than two hours: two hours that felt like an eternity. Finally, the phone rang.

"Is this Detective Callahan?" asked Schuster with an angst-ridden tone to his voice.

"Yes, it is," said Callahan, glancing at the ceiling with relief.

"This is Arnie Schuster."

In a soft, easygoing tone, Callahan replied, acknowledging him as a police officer, hoping to ease any possible tension. "I'm glad you called, brother."

"Yes, I know what you're talking about. This has bothered me for years," said Schuster. "I will cooperate fully."

"To make sure we understand each other, I am calling you because we know that you are aware of the murder of Morris Jackson by your friends Willy Mulgrew and Bobby Avilla."

"Yes, I understand."

"Can you come up tomorrow?"

"If I must, yes. But one thing, I hope the City will pick up the tab. We don't make shit down here."

"No problem," said Callahan. "We'll even pick you up and drop you off at LaGuardia and treat you to a first-class meal."

By noon the next day, Schuster was sitting in the back seat of the car with Callahan at his side. Roberts drove while Hartigan rode shotgun. As they crossed the busy Triborough Bridge to the Major Deegan Expressway, they talked shop, comparing crime in Miami and New York. In 1980 Miami experienced over 600 murders compared to New York City's 2,000 murders, which was the norm at the time. It was a thirty-five-minute ride to the precinct.

It wasn't long after they took seats in the squad room—with coffees and donuts of course—when Schuster began his story.

"On Christmas Eve, 1977," he said, "I was standing on the corner outside the London Lounge when Willy Mulgrew and Bobby Avilla pulled up in Bobby's red Mustang. They invited me to go along with them for a ride. Mulgrew said they were out to waste a dirtbag. I told them I had a party to go to and said goodbye. The next day I met Bobby again and he gave me a detailed account of what happened, acting like it was no big deal. 'There was hardly anybody on the streets, any dirtbags that is,' he said."

Callahan stopped him right there. "What did they mean by *dirtbags?*"

"I was going to explain," he said. "A black guy or Puerto Rican."

Schuster continued, "From there they drove up to Fordham Road and the Grand Concourse where Mulgrew fired at one target, a kid with a blasting boom box, but missed. The lucky kid probably never heard the shot, just kept on walking. They then cruised by Fordham University before stopping at a White Castle. After feeding their faces they resumed the hunt. It didn't take long before they spotted a target. That's when Mulgrew climbed into the back seat and removed the rifle from the duffle bag and opened the window. Avilla pulled up across the street and stopped. Then Willy aimed the rifle and fired a single shot."

"Did it hit Jackson?" asked Callahan.

"Yes," said Schuster.

Schuster continued, "I met Willy again a couple of days later in the London Lounge. He was still bragging about what he did. He passed around a newspaper clipping, I think it was the *Daily News*. I'm not sure. He passed it around to all his friends."

"Was it that "The Ghost of Christmas Past" thing?" asked Hartigan.

"Sounds like it. But that's a long time ago," said Schuster.

"Finally, things are starting to gel," said Hartigan. "Arnie, you are a big help to us. As you know, you'll have to testify."

Schuster replied, "Yes. It has been on my mind. I've been carrying this guilt far too long."

CHAPTER EIGHTEEN

MARCH 8, 1984 – "Time to move on," said Roberts while covering a yawn. "Let's start work on the second list. The known criminals. We'll check some rap sheets.

"The first name on the list of bad guys is Eric Stoneberg. This guy works in his family's delicate and would probably own it if he kept clean."

But as a kid, he wasn't too bright. He got involved with drugs. Per his police records, he never did anything good: drugs, robbery, and burglary: all to keep him supplied with drugs.

"Had better see what he knows," said Callahan with a suspicious look in his eyes. "I don't want to hear any more of that, 'I don't know anything bullshit.'"

Stoneberg perked up when he saw the three of them enter the mini-market. Callahan flashed his shield as he motioned him over to the end of the counter. Eric signaled his co-worker to take over.

"Why are you guys here?" he snapped, with an air of confrontation.

Callahan could see that he was on weed; his glassy, bloodshot eyes were dilated.

"Not for marijuana," said Callahan. "Why don't you step outside with us?" Once out on the street, Callahan got right to the point. "You know something about a murder. I want you to tell us all about it."

Real cocky like, Stoneberg replied, "I don't know diddlysquat about any fucking murder and I don't want to talk to you."

"Tell you what. We don't want to make a big scene here in front of your people. Instead, when your head clears up, meet us at the 48th tomorrow morning," said Callahan. "And don't forget. Don't make us come after you."

"I'll have the same fuck you attitude. But I will be there," said Eric, who made an abrupt about-face and walked into the store.

"In the good old days, I'd whack a nightstick right across his ass," said Hartigan.

"And in the good old days, he would say 'yes, sir' instead of 'fuck you'."

* * * * *

That night Ron Hartigan and his wife were at their favorite neighborhood restaurant with some friends enjoying each other's company over dinner and a couple of drinks. They chatted as the pianist tickled the ivories ever so softly in the background playing "Born Free". Ron was in the middle of a joke when a friend from the bar approached him with a message: "Ron, you got a phone call at the bar. Somebody named Callahan." Hartigan thanked him and headed to the bar.

"Yo, Tom. What you got?" said Hartigan into the receiver.

"Hope you're not in the middle of eating," said Callahan, who sounded upbeat.

"No. It will be a while yet before we eat," said Ron taking a sip of his scotch on the rocks. "So, what you got?"

"I'm sitting here staring at the boob tube, but thinking about Jackson ... and suddenly it dawns on me," he paused then raising his voice, said, "I just realized we never checked to see if a .22 rifle is registered to Willy Mulgrew or to his family."

Hartigan arched his eyebrows. "It's a good thing somebody's on the ball. Why didn't we think of that sooner? Tell you what, Tom, tomorrow as soon as we finish with Stoneberg, we'll head downtown to the Firearms Control Board and check it out."

"I got something too. I don't know if it pertains to us or not, but we'll find out soon enough. I ran into my cousin BB at the bar. He said there had been a killing tonight not far from the London Lounge. They found a DOA in the trunk of a car. Shot in the head."

* * * * *

MARCH 9, 1984 -- "I expected Eric here at nine," said Hartigan, who was behind his desk filing his fingernails, as he checked recent reports.

"Well it's obvious he's going to be late. If he shows up at all. It's already twenty-five past nine," said Roberts, an annoyed look on his face. "I hate that crap. No respect at all these days. These punks treat us like shit."

Callahan smiled. "As my father used to say, "Every dog has his day." That's when the phone rang and Callahan picked it up. "This you, Tom?" a voice on the other end asked.

"Yeah, BB?"

"Yep. You know a guy named Eric Stoneberg?"

"That's right. Why did you lock him up?" asked Callahan in a casual tone.

"No. I found his card … I mean your card, in his wallet."

Callahan asked, "What did he do?"

"Nothing. He's dead. He's the guy I told you about last night. The body we found in the trunk of the car: two bullets in the head. Apparently, a drug deal gone bad," said BB.

"Whoa. We were supposed to interview him this morning." He paused then thanked BB for the update.

Callahan stood. "Hey guys, that was my cousin at Homicide. Stoneberg's dead ... with two holes in his head."

"Shit, that's another potential witness gone," said Hartigan. By then Hartigan had finished filing his fingernails. "And the priest. I mean it was so long ago. Could he really be positive that was Mulgrew's picture?"

Hartigan checked the second list for the next name. "Let's go check this guy, Mulberry. See what we can get from this bird."

"Probably the same old *fuck you* tough guy shit," said Roberts, cracking a smile.

* * * * *

"This just came in," said Hartigan. "A supermarket up on Van Cortlandt Park South was hit by a lone perp...wielding a shotgun."

"I know exactly where that is," said Roberts. "A corner joint right across from the reservoir. I'll drive."

"That's still a decent neighborhood," said Callahan.

"Good. We can kill two birds with one stone. We'll check out the holdup, then pay a visit to Mulberry. See what we can get out of him," said Hartigan.

They jumped on the Cross-Bronx Expressway, which was right out front of the police station, headed west then looped on to the Major Deegan heading north for a few miles. They exited at Van Cortlandt Park East then drove to the top of the hill. They were at the supermarket in twenty minutes. Two patrol cars with their emergency lights still flashing were parked outside.

The Bronx Robbery Squad entered the store and were immediately updated on what had transpired by the patrol officers. "A lone, white male held up the store with a shotgun." They then spoke to the manager who filled them in on other details. He said he had seen the gunman before in the neighborhood and that he kept letting shoppers go before him. The gunman was waiting for when there was nobody checking out and then struck, pulling out a sawed-off shotgun from a bag in his cart. The manager also noticed that he kept chewing Hershey bars and dropping the wrappings into his wagon.

"We want to see the wagon," said Hartigan. He wanted to see the wrappings for possible fingerprints.

"Come. I put it in the back," he replied. The manager was still a bit nervous.

"Just great," said Roberts. "You didn't touch the wrappers, did you?"

"Nope. They're still in the wagon."

"You check it out, Tom," said Hartigan.

The manager took Callahan to the rear of the store, into the office where he had placed the shopping cart. They took a paper bag from the supermarket in which he put the wrappers, sealed, and labeled the bag, marking them with his initials. They were forwarded to Latent Prints.

* * * * *

When they finished with the supermarket holdup, they responded to Reservoir Avenue near the Jerome Park Reservoir looking for Jake Mulberry from their known criminal list. Better known as The Mole, Mulberry was a drug dealer—often guys became dealers to ease their own addictions--an addict, and a burglar. He was a good friend of Mulgrew and often drank with him in the London Lounge.

They spotted The Mole in a schoolyard with a couple of friends. Separating them was a twelve-foot-high chain link fence that enclosed one side of the yard. Knowing which one was Mulberry from mug shots, Callahan shouted through the fence, "Hey, Mulberry, we'd like to talk to you." He was about twenty feet from them. He moved to about five or six feet from the fence that separated him from Callahan.

"What do you guys want with me?" he asked, knowing well that they were detectives, which at that time Callahan informed him officially, "Concerning a murder you have knowledge about."

"You're out of your fucking mind," shouted Mulberry, while stepping up to the fence and flexing his broad chest and muscular biceps as if challenging Callahan. "I have nothing to say to you or your friends. So, go fuck yourself and leave me alone."

"You ought to be polite, a little shit like you. You wait there. I am coming around to talk to you," he said, maintaining his cool. Callahan, Roberts, and Hartigan entered the schoolyard and approached Mulberry. As they neared him, Hartigan whispered, "Don't lose it, Tom." Hartigan then directed Mulberry's friends to back off. They obeyed reluctantly, grumbling as they did.

Callahan closed in on him; he tapped his nose several times with a pencil. "Don't get so excited. We just want to talk to you, big guy."

Pushing the pencil away, Mulberry shouted, "About what!"

"About a homicide!"

Mulberry shouted again, "I don't know shit about any murder committed by anybody. So, leave me the fuck alone."

"You're going to talk to us one way or the other. This is not going away. A young man was murdered for no reason and you know the details as told to you by the murderer."

"Like I said, I don't know shit about no murder."

"Okay, you don't want to talk here. So now you can tell your story to a Grand Jury." With that Callahan pulled the subpoena from his suit jacket.

Once Mulberry saw the subpoena, he became highly agitated, spouting expletives as fast as he could get them out. When Callahan filled out the subpoena, Mulberry brushed past him to get away, but not before Callahan spotted a shiny object attached to his waistband. With that, they stopped him and frisked him. The shiny object turned out to be a cigarette case and lighter holder attached to his belt.

Callahan served him the subpoena due for the next day, March 10, 1984.

On arriving at the 48th, Callahan went right to Latent Prints where he dropped off the candy wrappers. Sure enough, there were fingerprints. "Once we get this guy's details, we'll go look for him," said the boss.

The phone rang. It was for Callahan. He pulled away from the receiver and shouted, "Whoa, whoa. Hold it up. Who is this?"

It was Mulberry's mother. She poured out several nasty expletives, cursing Callahan out for involving her son in a murder. Callahan said he'd like to talk to her if that would be okay. She agreed. He and his partners went to her house and served her a subpoena, not to coincide with her son's.

CHAPTER NINETEEN

L ater that afternoon Callahan was contacted by Latent Prints, which was next door to them. Good news, but bad news. A search of the prints produced the name, Charles Duprey and the perp's address. *Hell, I know that name. Charlie Duprey. Wonder if there is any connection?* They pulled his photo and rap sheet from Intelligence; he was a junkie, a small-time dealer, and a stickup man. Callahan had known a Duprey family that lived on his old block when he was a youngster.

When Mrs. Mulberry subsequently went before the Assistant District Attorney, Ross Mantoso, she very aggressively complained about the detectives harassing her son. Mantoso gave her a stern warning that she was interfering with the law and could be arrested and prosecuted. Further, that these detectives that she held with such contempt because of her darling criminal son, were dedicated men determined to find those responsible for the racist killing of a young man who'd harmed no one, and who had the full support of the District Attorney. Her lips moved as she, "Ah, ah, ah'd," but said nothing else.

Hartigan added, "You might want to know that the young man who was killed had just left Midnight Mass at Fordham . . . God rest his soul."

* * * * *

MARCH 12, 1984 – Nobody responded to Callahan's loud pounding on Charles Duprey's flimsy outside basement door. Hartigan rapped on the adjoining windows that faced the side yard of the private dwelling where he lived. It was a turn of the century, poorly maintained, wood-frame building. After five or more minutes of knocking and getting no response, they moved on to check out some neighborhood drug stops. No luck there either. But their appearance got the pushers to move on.

Just when they were about to give up for the day, Hartigan decided to return to Duprey's home for one more attempt to locate him. That's when they spotted the familiar face of a young lady sitting on the stoop next to Duprey. She was sitting with a young man who reminded Callahan of Charlie Duprey, who he'd known in the old days. Upon questioning, they determined that he was Charles Duprey. They braced him to prevent him from escaping. He offered no resistance.

They booked him for armed robbery at Bronx Robbery. Callahan chose to question him because of his last name. Right away he learned that his father was Charlie Duprey. He learned, too, that his father had died of a drug overdose one night on a park bench.

Callahan knew the family from the old neighborhood. Young Duprey's uncles, Peter and John went to the same school as Callahan. Charles, Duprey's father, got hooked on drugs and became a criminal. Peter went on to the Merchant Marine Academy. John worked in construction.

Duprey was resigned to a life of drugs. He had no fear of prison.

Callahan told young Duprey he might be able to help him out with the DA, but Charles Duprey declined any help preferring to be incarcerated to get cleaned up and off the drugs.

Through the grapevine several years later, Callahan learned that young Charles Duprey also died of an overdose. Like father like son.

* * * * *

APRIL 15, 1984 -- The squad got another big break when they arrested Tony Moore for drug-related offenses. He was willing to talk frankly hoping that the DA would cut him some slack in sentencing.

After they read him his Miranda rights, he made the following statement.

"My cousin JP Lonnigan told me to be careful, that Santos was a rat. I said why? He told me because he knew Willy Mulgrew killed someone seven years ago. Said he asked Willy what happened and he told me that in 1977 when he was tripping on acid he shot a black guy for being black. I asked him if he was arrested and he told me no. He also told me that Bobby Avilla was the only witness and that he drove the car. Also, that Avilla threw away the gun. I also spoke to his brother Pat Mulgrew a few weeks after it happened and told him it was messed up about his brother. He said yes, but everything would be all right if Avilla kept his mouth shut."

Continuously scratching his head and tapping his foot on the floor, it was obvious Moore did not like ratting on his friends. He even said, "I hate doing this, but my ass is more important than his."

Early in May, the decision was made to start serving subpoenas to even more of the people on the lists. By then the squad was certain of the identity of the many people Mulgrew and Avilla had told of their cowardly deed. Two weeks later they entered the London Lounge and subpoenaed the bartender, Benny Rivera. By the end of May, they had subpoenaed seven people including a voluntary witness, Mrs. Schroeder, the mother of Avilla's common-law wife. Mrs. Schroeder was afraid for the safety of her and her daughter. Avilla had told her daughter about the killing, which she then told her mother. She testified before the Grand Jury on February 29, 1984, when she provided the details of the murder as told to her by her daughter, including the fact that Avilla at the time owned a red car. That month they served subpoenas to two more of Mulgrew and Avilla's bar friends, Earl Schmutz, and Jane Lonnigan, JP Lonnigan's wife. She was present at the meeting at the Lonnigan's apartment.

That day they also picked up Mulgrew's mother at her place of work to transport her to the Grand Jury where she gave sworn testimony that she once had access to a .22-caliber rifle registered to her husband who no longer lived with her. They verified that information through the Firearms Control Board down at One Police Plaza. Now they knew that Willy Mulgrew had access to a .22-caliber rifle. They also learned that one of Mulgrew's friends, a Marine named Sanchez, had borrowed the weapon three years ago to kill his drill instructor. Fortunately, Sanchez was discharged before he could carry out his deadly deed. Mulgrew told him to get rid of the weapon, which he did. He threw it into a river in South Carolina, not too far from the Marine base.

Sanchez, trying to put his life together, would eventually testify.

The last person they were to subpoena for the next day's Grand Jury was Mulgrew's best friend, the tough kid JP. They surprised him at his apartment. Once again Callahan, the case officer, took the lead. "Tell us what you know about the murder?" Lonnigan's response and disposition were the same as they were at the first interview. He said he knew nothing about any murder and again told them to "go fuck yourselves" and to leave him alone. Callahan, with cold, suspicious eyes staring into Lonnigan's, told him, "If you don't want to talk to us, maybe you will talk to the Grand Jury." With a smile, Callahan served him the subpoena for the following day, to join the others in the courtroom. All Lonnigan could do was stutter.

"It's time to talk to Mulgrew," said Hartigan, suggesting they cruise the neighborhood to try to find him. "We need to find this guy. To feel him out. See what he has to say."

* * * * *

So, they did a slow drive through of the neighborhood looking for him, starting at the corner of the Jerome Avenue and Kingsbridge Road, and headed west. They passed Bonner's shop, then parked across the street outside the Veterans' Hospital grounds that were opposite the London Lounge where they waited and watched. After thirty minutes or so they moved on, no sign of Mulgrew. From there they drove through the streets around Kingsbridge Road. It wasn't until they approached the neighborhood firehouse that they saw him talking to a fireman in front of the firehouse. They pulled up on the apron. Callahan called Mulgrew aside and requested that he take a ride. They wanted to talk to him, to which he complied. After the proper identifications, during which Mulgrew said, "I know damn well who you guys are." Callahan advised him that he was not under arrest, but still read him his Miranda rights.

"Willy, do you know what we want to talk to you about?" asked Callahan, who was taking the lead. He stared hard into Mulgrew's eyes.

"Nope," Mulgrew answered, feigning a puzzled look.

"How come you went to the Fiftieth Precinct to see Detective Ed Hanson and told him that a detective named Callahan was looking for you for some homicide?" Callahan continued.

Mulgrew replied, "The junkies are trying to frame me. You know I'm probably the only guy in this neighborhood that gives a fuck. I'm an upstanding citizen. I've even turned in bad guys to the Department."

Right then the warning bells of the firehouse overhead doors started sounding and the doors opened. Half a dozen firefighters ran out to the sidewalk and the street to control traffic. The car jerked as Roberts hit the gas and brake at the same time as he moved the car out of the way. The sirens wailed as the trucks rolled out into traffic and picked up the firemen, then sped off.

"Have you ever been arrested?" Callahan continued.

"Yes," said Mulgrew. "For throwing rocks at a bus."

They looked each other in the eye, Callahan with a slight smile and Mulgrew with a defiant look.

"That's all?" Callahan's look hardened.

"Yep."

"Weren't you arrested for burglary?" Callahan continued.

"Oh**,**" he laughed. "That was a long time ago."

"That still counts. Were you not busted for possession of a .357 Magnum?"

"Yep. That too was a long time ago."

"So, you have been arrested before? For serious offenses?"

Mulgrew was irked by the questions. He challenged Callahan's questioning. "So, what? What's all this bullshit about? I never hurt anyone in my life."

Hartigan cut in. "What do you think, Willy? Somebody made all this shit up?"

Mulgrew glared at Hartigan then turned to Callahan and answered, "All I do is help people, and this is the shit I get. They questioned me about the dead police officer in the reservoir. They questioned me about a homicide on the Deegan. Everybody blames everything on me when you assholes can't get your man. I've probably made more citizens arrests than the three of you have made collars."

"Willy, let's stop the bullshit and get down to business here. I think you know well what we are talking about. And by the way, did they question you about five derelicts shot dead on the subway and in Van Cortlandt Park?"

"I don't know what you're talking about," he said, raising his voice. "I help people, and I am not a racist. I help blacks and Hispanics. I am a good Irish guy. I was taught good by my parents."

Callahan continued, "Then how do you think all of this came about? Do you think it was all made up?"

This time he grinned. "I told you, the junkies are trying to set me up."

"You hang out with users? Ain't that right?" said Callahan. "So, why are your buddies trying to set you up?"

"Look I helped you guys. I carried a scanner. I responded to many crime scenes--probably over two hundred or more."

"You ever respond to a homicide when you were a teenager, back on Christmas Eve 1977? In front of Fordham University?" asked Callahan, staring hard into his eyes looking for his reaction. Still a defiant look.

"Nope."

"Do you know Bobby Avilla?"

"Yeah," he said, pulling his head back slightly.

"Is he a stand-up guy?"

Callahan kept his suspicious-looking eyes trained on Mulgrew's making him a bit uneasy.

"How do I know? You know you guys must think I'm a real asshole." He shifted his eyes from Callahan to Roberts to Hartigan, then back to Callahan. "I know you guys have that Donny Santos and Tony Moore, and a few other guys, all wired up. I'm no jerk, I'm going on the Job." He meant he was going to join the police.

"You think you're going on the Job? I don't think so," said Callahan, shaking his head.

"We'll see about that, but I'll tell you this, I'm going to sue the three of you and IAD will have a case on you." He smirked.

"Anything else you want to say, Willy? Here's my card with my name and number. Call me if you change your mind." Callahan grinned.

"Fuck you," he said, as he stepped out of the car.

Callahan wasn't finished. "You know, Willy, one day we are going to arrest you for murder." This set Willy Mulgrew into an angry tirade. First, he cursed them out with some nasty invectives.

He then challenged their abilities as detectives. He said, "I've made more arrests than the three of you guys put together," baffling them. With that, Mulgrew walked away smiling. They all agreed simultaneously. The three of them agreed je was a psycho.

"What is he talking about?" asked Roberts, while scratching his head.

"One more thing, Pyro," said Callahan, who then paused awaiting Mulgrew's response.

He turned back, losing his smile that was replaced with a startled look, but said nothing.

Callahan continued, "Did you ever get pulled in for arson?"

CHAPTER TWENTY

Over the life of the investigation, the detectives had gotten to know both individuals quite intimately. Willy was an enigma-intelligent, psychotic, and a detestable person, but likable. Avilla was the opposite: not likable.

They had learned too, a lot more about Morris Jackson. By doing background checks and interviews with Morris Jackson's friends, a person evolved, a very decent person, well-liked. He was actively involved in obtaining college scholarships for inner-city youths and influencing the young men and women to take advantage of the opportunities.

As time passed, they'd learned a lot about Mulgrew. In the words of one of his associates, he was a "rat bastard". That was verified by Detective Hanson from the 46th Precinct. Mulgrew was a Confidential Informant for several detectives.

More than one person had volunteered shocking information about Mulgrew; that he had bragged about killing "lowlifes" in the early hours of the morning, derelicts who'd been sleeping in parks or on subway cars. He'd often dress like a woman when going on the hunt. A couple of the informants even said that Mulgrew had asked them to join him on the hunts. He also took pop shots at buildings where minority members lived. On one occasion, he fired several shots into a restaurant that was open for business. He even considered killing his partner in murder, Bobby Avilla, to keep him quiet, having feared he would rat him out.

Others also said that he was an arsonist and a fire buff—that he watched the fires he had set—that he had set several fires in his former residence, one of the larger apartment complexes in the neighborhood. He also set fire to several other residential and commercial buildings in the neighborhood.

Per fire reports obtained by the squad from the fire department and based on information provided Callahan by his firefighter friend Lieutenant Fatima, who had worked at many of the fires, several of which were major fires at which he saw Mulgrew.

One of the informants, a guy named Tobby Mueller, told the detectives, that he once went with Willy to a local gas station where Willy filled two one-gallon bottles with gasoline which he placed in a cloth shopping bag. They then went to one of the apartment buildings Mulgrew had lived in. The informant said he did not know what Willy was up to.

They took the elevator to the top floor where he followed Willy to a vacant apartment. Callahan asked, "How did he know where the vacant apartment was?"

"I don't know," said Mueller the informant.

"Why did you go with him?"

"I was afraid of the guy. I did what he said. He was crazy," said Mueller.

"What then," said Callahan.

"He soaked two rooms with the gasoline had big holes in the ceilings. I wondered how and when he made the holes. Knowing he was crazy; I chose not to ask. But I did ask what the hell are you up to? And when he said he was going to set the place on fire, I took off like a bat out of hell. I started down the stairs two steps at a time. I hurried out to the street. When I looked up and saw flames shooting out three windows, I took off."

Callahan snarled, "Did you think to call the fire department?"

Muller was quick to respond, "Yes."

Not long after he started the fire, Mulgrew was on the roof of another building watching a major fire with flame and heavy, thick smoke shooting from many windows.

Little did Mulgrew know, he was seen by Lieutenant Fatima who was working the fire. He told Callahan he had previously seen Mulgrew at other major fires and that he always seemed excited, like he enjoyed the fires.

Willy Mulgrew was a military enthusiast. He kept up a subscription to *Soldier of Fortune.* He also possessed a collection of military manuals, which from time to time he found a use for.

A strange man he was. Mulgrew liked a certain young lady from the neighborhood who was interested in another neighborhood guy, a personal acquaintance. This young fellow owned a well-maintained blue convertible. As word had it, Mulgrew learned about an easy-to-make metal-destroying-acid, used by the military against the enemy, of course. But he decided to use it against his competition. He went ahead and made up the solution and one night applied it to the blue convertible.

During a discussion one day, Mulgrew's friend told him about his car and how it suddenly began falling apart. And what was Mulgrew's response? Do you park the car near the beach when you go to Rockaway? It's probably the salt in the air.

* * * * *

JUNE 18, 1984 -- Almost three months after Jake Mulberry was subpoenaed, Detective Callahan received a call from Mulberry's wife, stating that they would like to meet with the detectives and provide them with additional information. Mrs. Mulberry stated, "Her husband does not want to be mixed up in the Mulgrew homicide case." An hour later the Mulberrys arrived at Bronx Robbery where Jake Mulberry related the following information. Present for the interview was Detectives Callahan and Roberts.

"I was told directly by Mulgrew about the Jackson homicide. About five years ago, Mulgrew said to me, 'I shot a nigger in the back over on Fordham.' I heard the same thing from other people, but could not remember exactly who told me. I also heard from him directly that he had shot other people and killed them."

Callahan stopped him. "Who is the him you're referring to?"

"Mulgrew," said Mulberry.

"When you say Mulgrew, you mean William Mulgrew. Is that correct?" said Callahan. Mulberry nodded his agreement.

"I was also present in Mulgrew's apartment this summer when Mulgrew told me he felt he was going to be arrested shortly for killing Jackson. He told me that he felt he could trust me. Said I was not like the others who were all ratting him out, especially Santos. He was also cleaning out his room. He gave me a shopping bag full of books on firearms and other related matter. Mulgrew told me not to let them get into any other person's hands. Mulgrew's brother Frank and his girlfriend were in the room at the time. I took the books to my mother's house. She said she would get rid of them.

"Soon after Willy was arrested, Frank Mulgrew drove me to Rikers Island to visit Willy at his request. Willy was highly disturbed that his friends had given him up. He discussed taking a plea that would include Avilla getting off easier. When we were leaving, we passed Avilla who shouted, "Tell Santos that he was as good as dead." After Frank Mulgrew and I returned from Rikers, we parted by the reservoir where he discussed his brother's situation. I remember clearly Frank telling me, 'That's what happens to you when you're a murderer'."

Mulberry had a real change of heart about his friend. He was really unloading on Mulgrew. He went on to discuss an unrelated Mulgrew matter. As the squad had heard several times during their interviews with Mulgrew's friends, Mulgrew's nickname was Pyro, and he liked to set fires. Mulberry closed out his commentary, "At one time I was present in a car with him, a few years ago, the date I cannot remember, when he wanted me to burn down a bar, which I did not want to do. Yet I felt compelled to do it for Mulgrew. He had a strange power over a lot of people. And you felt like he was crazy enough to come after you for any little thing, never mind tattling on him. I left the car and went to the rear of the bar and pretended to set a fire.

"I then came out and got in the car, which we parked a distance away with the bar in view so that Willy could watch for flames. After a while, when it was obvious there was no fire, Mulgrew became upset with me, calling me a pussy. That I had no balls."

* * * * *

JUNE 23, 1984--Good things were happening with the Mulgrew/Avilla case. On this day, they got a call from Mulberry's mother, Mrs. Celia Mulberry. Callahan answered the phone as the case was officially assigned to him even though Roberts and Hartigan worked hand and hand with him.

"This is Detective Callahan. How can I help you, Mrs. Mulberry?"

"I would like you to come to my apartment and pick up books and magazines my son got from Mulgrew when he went to his apartment," she said.

"What kind of magazines and books are they?" Callahan asked.

"Some of them are *Soldier of Fortune*. The others are some kind of army manuals."

"All right, we'll be there about three. Okay?"

She agreed with the time, then provided her address.

CHAPTER TWENTY-ONE

JULY 9, 1984 -- Finally, after a year-long investigation, the squad had their indictments of Mulgrew and Avilla. All they needed now were the arrest warrants from the DA, and they came swiftly. When the District Attorney learned that Presidential Candidate Walter Mondale would shortly announce his choice of Queens Congresswoman Geraldine Ferraro, as a running-mate—the first woman ever to be selected for such a high post—she would dominate the news media for the next couple of weeks. If that happened, the arrests of the two racial murderers would be buried, giving the DA very little media coverage. In New York, the DA was elected, and he needed the people to see that he was doing his job, being tough on crime and supporting justice for the black kids. He wanted to be sure that he got the headlines before the Congresswoman.

The following evening, to preempt the Ferraro announcement, the District Attorney ordered the immediate arrests of Mulgrew and Avilla. As soon as Bronx Robbery was notified to carry out the arrests, the officer on duty called Roberts and Callahan into his office. The OIC, Lt. Dallas, explained the situation and asked, "Would you be able to make the arrests tonight?"

"No problem at all," said Detective Lew Roberts.

"We have to get Hartigan in for this," said Callahan. "He's been organizing this investigation since day one." Dallas agreed. Hartigan arrived in plenty of time to lead the arrest squad.

The detectives knew exactly where the two of them would be that night: Avilla would be working in a local liquor store, and Mulgrew would be at home till he headed out to the London Lounge.

But before they would do anything that might cause Mrs. Sarah Jackson any further pain or upset, they wanted to be the first to break the news to her about the arrests of Mulgrew and Avilla for the murder of her son. They did not want her to experience the shock of learning about it through the news media.

It was after 7 PM when they arrived at her home in Queens. She had just finished having dinner with her son Paul, also a police officer, who had been visiting. Of course, the squad would have waited for the following morning, but the DA's wishes were the priority. He wanted this racially-motivated cold-case homicide to be given maximum publicity. Besides the publicity, which would be very helpful toward his reelection bid, he also wanted to throw the book at Mulgrew.

Morris Jackson's mother was startled when she opened the door and saw the three detectives standing there. She had no idea of why they were there. After the detectives identified themselves, she thought maybe they wanted to see her son, Paul, the police officer. It was when they asked if her husband was home that they learned that he had since passed away.

The detectives had not been in touch with Mrs. Jackson during their investigation. They knew she would not be able to help them since Morris had been a random victim and they did not want to open up old memories and pain until they had something positive to tell her.

Sergeant Ron Hartigan was the spokesman. "We have some very important news concerning Morris's death. Tonight, we will arrest the two men responsible."

When they explained that the killing was racially-motivated, she wept and called out to Jesus. Her son embraced her while the others sought to console her. They told her of all the kind words said about her son, about how truly dedicated he was to helping others get on the path to success, which was confirmed by different teachers and professors at Fordham University. They emphasized how popular he was with his fellow students.

Once she calmed herself, she explained the reason for her outburst. It had always been her belief that someone who knew Morris had killed him and that that someone would also kill his brother.

* * * * *

An hour later the detectives pulled up in front of Zak's Liquors. They could see the startled look on Avilla's face as he watched them exit the car. He knew what arriving at this hour meant. As Callahan led the men into the store, Avilla shouted, "Why don't you guys leave me the fuck alone?" Callahan continued to the back of the counter, almost touching him. "Time's up, Bobby," he shouted. "Robert Avilla, I am placing you under arrest for the murder of Morris Jackson."

"This is bullshit," shouted Avilla, acting the badass. A slap across the face silenced him. Callahan cuffed his hands as he read him his Miranda rights.

They led the stunned Avilla out of the store, placed him in the back seat of the car where Callahan joined him. Lew Roberts and Ron Hartigan rode up front. They took him to Bronx Robbery, placed him in a holding cell. Another detective began processing him.

The trio promptly returned to the neighborhood to arrest Mulgrew whose routine they knew by heart after so often waiting outside his residence watching for him. They often sat there for long periods during which time they sometimes looked skyward as if praying, calling out, "Morris, will you please make him appear," which sometimes he did.

Such calls to Morris Jackson became part of their routine. "It was like he was one of us," said Hartigan. Sure enough, at 11:05 Mulgrew, wearing a camouflage baseball cap—oddly enough he wasn't wearing his *Police Brutality Is the Best Part of Police Work*

T-shirt—stepped out of his apartment building. At the same time, the squad stepped out of the shadows and surrounded him.

"Not you guys again," he shouted. "Leave me the fuck –"

"Save it," shouted Callahan. "William Mulgrew, we are placing you under arrest for the murder of Morris Jackson." Once again, Callahan used his cuffs, securing the perp's hands behind his back. He read him his Miranda rights as they led him to the car. Like Avilla, Callahan joined him in the back seat; the others took the front seats. They returned to Bronx Robbery where they booked him.

After completing the initial paperwork and making the proper notifications, they took the two perps to Central Booking about 5AM where they were processed and held for arraignment, fingerprinting, and photos. The following morning, after filing an Unusual Circumstance Report and making all the proper notifications to their superiors including the department's press liaison and DA's office, the three robbery detectives took them in handcuffs via the Perp Walk, with heavy media coverage, to the Bronx Supreme Court. The massive publicity they received pissed off many a friend in homicide. Mulgrew and Avilla were arraigned for murder with bail set at $1,000,000.

Afterward, they were turned over to the Department of Corrections where they would spend the next year in a segregated section of the prison, where the "celebrities" were housed. "Celebrities" that joined them during that year included Bernie Getz—known for attacking his attackers on a subway in December 1984; Christopher Thomas—known as the Palm Sunday Killer from a mass-murder in Brooklyn in April 1984 that included children; and others.

* * * * *

It was still daylight when the press conference commenced outside the 48th Precinct. All the news media and police brass were present, and, of course, the top echelons of the Bronx District Attorney's Office. Their vehicles filled the street, it had to be closed off. The trio of detectives stood beside the DA and the police brass. They were surrounded by an army of news media personalities and their camera crews.

The District Attorney praised the three detectives by name, Thomas Callahan, Louis Roberts, and Ron Hartigan for their persistence in penetrating the seven years of silence that had long surrounded this cold case. He labeled the murder as racist charging that both Mulgrew and Avilla hated blacks and Puerto Ricans. It should be noted that Avilla was a Cuban, a Hispanic. Per the team of detectives who investigated the cold case, allegedly much of that hatred stemmed from the stabbing death of one of their friends on a city bus "by a member of a minority group."

Both the Chief of Detectives and Chief of Detectives Bronx, expressed high admiration for the team, highlighting the many hours of their own time put into the case, often neglecting their families and emphasizing how they had started their investigation with nothing to work with yet they persisted and were successful. They demonstrated excellent police investigating that would continue for another year. The brass also emphasized the threats they received and the taunts from the people in the neighborhood, even an attempt on Callahan's life when somebody planted a homemade explosive device in his car.

After the DA and the Chiefs delivered their prepared statements, the press conference was opened for questions from the media. One reporter noted that a Catholic priest gave Jackson Last Rites. The priest quoted Morris' last words, "Tell my family I love them". It was after the questioning of the brass that Roberts, Hartigan, and Callahan were each interviewed by all the media, *New York Post, Daily News* and *New York Times* and all the major TV networks of the time.

A leading *Fox News* personality and her crew were in the process of shutting down when Lew Roberts started talking about how they would routinely talk to Morris Jackson, the victim, while staking out the two alleged killers. "We often referred to Jackson as the Fourth Detective on the case." Roberts's comment got their attention, and they decided to record it. "When we were on stakeout we would often call out Morris Jackson's name as if talking to him, and ask him, to do us a favor and get him out of the house which sometimes happened almost right away."

* * * * *

After the press conference the Assistant District Attorney, Ross Mantoso, requested the detectives and members of his staff to attend a strategy meeting on the following morning. He wanted to build a case that would find these alleged killers guilty, not just to indict them. An indictment is very different from a conviction. Before a jury sends a person to jail for twenty-five plus years, they must be convinced of his guilt. In a normal case, there are usually eyewitnesses, physical evidence, and possibly an incriminating statement from the defendant. In this case, there was no such evidence. This homicide was now almost eight years old.

At the meeting the following morning Mantoso outlined the problems he faced in obtaining a conviction. He also mentioned that a top trial lawyer, Oliver Fuscano, had been hired as Mulgrew's defense attorney. Fuscano was a well-known figure in the Bronx Court House. Capable, likable, and flamboyant were his trademarks. He drove to work every day in a white Rolls Royce, carried a walking stick, was always neatly dressed, and wore a fresh carnation in his lapel.

Fuscano loved being a lawyer and would probably be happy dying of a heart attack on the courtroom floor during a summation. He usually handled high-end cases. Organized crime, white collar, and political cases were his forte. He had already filed several motions and requests for hearings. The detectives could not figure out how Mulgrew could afford a lawyer of this caliber. Fuscano believed this was an open and closed case in Mulgrew's favor.

Mantoso outlined the strengths and weaknesses of the case and the alternatives. There were only two. He could offer Mulgrew a deal to plead guilty to a lesser crime, probably manslaughter, with a significantly reduced prison sentence, or go to trial with a weak case based on circumstantial and hearsay evidence. Everyone agreed to go to trial, which was Callahan, Hartigan, and Roberts' preference. The detectives were determined to nail him. They would attempt to garner additional testimony and evidence to assist in the prosecution. Of course, they lined up Father Michael Fahey who repeated his earlier story. They had Feeney's testament—though the man had died in prison earlier that year. There were some reluctant witnesses who testified that Mulgrew bragged about being the shooter in the *Daily News* article. And they had others to fill in pieces of the case as much as possible.

For the next several months they followed up on any lead and interviewed anybody who might have information on the case. For the most part, the information obtained duplicated what they already had. In one interview the person said he had asked Willy about the gun and was told that he gave it to a friend so he could kill his Marine drill instructor, which they had already heard from Sanchez.

The detectives eventually interviewed the individual who said that Willy Mulgrew had a .22 caliber rifle that he wanted to borrow to go hunting. He was in the Marine Corps at the time, he knew that if he asked Willy for the gun to go hunting, he would say no. So, he made up a story that he wanted to use the gun to kill his drill instructor. He had the gun in the trunk of his car when it was stolen from a parking lot in Virginia.

One day, out of the blue, the detectives received a message, Avilla wanted to talk to them. A meeting was set up. Avilla agreed to cooperate and testify against Willy Mulgrew if he were promised a reduced sentence. He was brought to Mantoso's office, with his lawyer present. A plea deal was made that he would plead guilty to manslaughter and testify against Mulgrew.

The trial that began in August, 1985 was attended by the detectives who watched as the witnesses presented evidence of Willy's racist rants, and as people spoke emotionally against the waste of Morris's life. And Avilla's testimony was the one that convinced the jury that this was premeditated and that Willy was proud of his actions, always showing the "The Ghost of Christmas Past," paper clipping.

Finally, after four weeks, the case was sealed, bringing relief to Mrs. Jackson's often tear-filled eyes. This was no longer a case based on hearsay evidence. This was hard eyewitness testimony from a co-conspirator.

Mrs. Jackson and her son Paul showed up daily at the trial. After the trial, Morris's mother reiterated her long-held fears for her younger son. Not knowing who or why Morris was killed or who killed him, her second son might face the same fate as his brother. Now she felt that this was no longer a concern. After Mulgrew's conviction, Morris's mother said that she could finally rest easy.

On September 30, 1985, the Bronx District Attorney announced that twenty-five-year-old Willy Mulgrew had been found guilty of Second-Degree Murder after a four-week trial of the murder of Morris Jackson on Christmas Eve after Midnight Mass at Fordham University in 1977.

On October 22, 1985, Mulgrew was sentenced to twenty-five years to life. In 2009, he became eligible for parole which was denied four times. He died in prison in 2015. Mulgrew was never charged with any other crime, including the rumored shooting of five derelicts and numerous alleged arson jobs.

Robert Avilla, who was with Mulgrew at the time of the killing, plead guilty to the charge of manslaughter and was sentenced to fifteen years. He was released from prison after four years and moved to Florida.

* * * * *

Even as Mulgrew and Avilla did their time, Sergeant Hartigan and Detectives Callahan and Roberts continued risking their lives while performing their duties as police officers.

Still, their main focus remained robbery, and they turned over any murder investigations to the homicide squad. This case had tested some of their bonds with their fellow officers, and they knew a "hot" case needed the full attention of the officers available.

The team of detectives responsible for resolving this cold case were highly praised by the media and received plenty of attention. 20/20 even did a segment on the case. Rightfully so. They had put much of their own time into this case while they carried on their own robbery work load. These men won many department awards and citations over their careers but this case was always very special. As Callahan said, speaking on behalf of his brothers in blue, it was about justice. And that's why they so often put their lives on the line.

Sadly, over the next decades, the influx of drugs, poverty, and crime kept them busy. The Bronx recovered a bit, but the troubles keep spreading, with drugs, dealers and the assorted crimes showing up in surrounding suburbs. There doesn't seem to be any way to stop the horrors of what comes with addiction, or the desperation of the men and woman ravaged by it.

When the media attention died down, they were left with an empty feeling. They had spent the past two years thinking about this case every day. Now there was a void. They became bored and though they did their jobs to the best of their ability, they rarely felt that urgency.

Hartigan was promoted to lieutenant and transferred to another command. Roberts transferred to the prestigious Bronx District Attorney's office. And though Callahan stayed with Robbery, he would retire a few years later on disability.

Yet they always stayed in touch, and would occasionally meet for lunch or dinner, remembering the days of Morris Jackson, a burning sense of justice, and "The Ghost of Christmas Past".

AFTERWORD

This case was inspired by the work of three brave, diligent and dedicated detectives.

Detectives Thomas Gallagher, Lewis Robeson, and Sergeant Ron Heffernan were working the Robbery division in the South Bronx in 1983 when a drug-addicted felon traded some info on a cold-case murder for a reduced sentence.

Little did they know that they'd be spending their spare time over the next eighteen months tracking down all the details of the case—starting with who was the victim, and finishing with a way to prove the case to the jury. They worked Robbery, not Homicide, but after learning of the senseless, racist actions of the killer, and the brilliant, outstanding, promising African-American man who was killed on Christmas Eve, they wouldn't rest until justice was done.

This is also the story of how the rise of drugs—the sale, the pursuit, the use and the pains of addiction—changed neighborhoods, pulling apart the bonds of community, the trust in family and neighbors and causing spikes in crime.

When drugs enter into a neighborhood, crime follows. Those who commit a crime to get money for more drugs, those who commit crimes while high on drugs, and those who commit crimes because they don't feel there is anything left to live for.

At the heart of the story, though, is the dogged persistence—almost obsession—of Gallagher, Robeson, and Heffernan. They attacked the case from multiple angles, never wavering in their commitment for justice for Michael Johnson, even before they learned who he was.

It was one of New York's first cold cases—seven years of not knowing who or why. And in the end, justice was done.

It's been forty years since the senseless death that started this story. Sadly, the pursuit of drugs is still leading to pain and suffering and crimes and violence. But there's some good news as well, as the South Bronx isn't burning anymore. There's nothing left to burn. But we're not safe yet.

Still, as long as there are Men in Blue like these three detectives who shared their experiences and insight with me, there is hope.